Full Service

Cora Rose

Copyright © 2024 by Cora Rose

All rights reserved.

No part of this book may be reproduced in any form or by any electronic or mechanical means, including information storage and retrieval systems, without written permission from the author, except for the use of brief quotations in a book review.

Editor: Angela O'Connell
Cover Design: Natasha Snow
Photographer: @xramragde

Chapter One

Silas

I've seen that ass before. I *know* I have. The way it bunches and flexes in those tight jeans. The round globes of each cheek. The way they bounce and move. I can tell even through the fabric of his pants. That's how obsessed I am.

Fuck. Me. I *know* that ass.

I tap my pen against my lips as the breeze flutters the quizzes I'm grading under my hand. I squint my eyes behind my slightly outdated sunglasses as I lean forward and examine it once more. Round, pert, completely biteable.

A perfect peach.

Unfortunately, said peach looks like it belongs to a student here on Franklin U's campus. Which makes this completely inappropriate.

I behaved abominably at a friend's bachelor party. Like a dog in heat. I don't even know why Chris insisted on going to a strip club in the first place. Probably because Gregory was with him and was the sole entertainer for his fiancé. I know for a fact

Gregory wouldn't let Chris within a mile of another half-naked man. His jealousy knows no bounds.

But as for me, I have no excuse for the way I behaved, even though I'm a true bachelor with years of lazy, can't-be-bothered celibacy under my belt. I got a lap dance from a young stripper who had moved like he was fucking his ass onto my dick.

It was the hottest experience of my life and one that I'm mostly ashamed of.

Never in my life have I come like that, not even as a teenager. It only took a few rolls of his hips and rubs from that butt on my weeping dick and I was done for. An abomination, a complete scoundrel. Jerking and grunting as I unloaded into my khaki dress pants.

That's me.

A thirty-five-year-old tenured professor coming to the mere thought of a student's ass sitting on me.

Well, to be fair, at the time, I didn't know he was a student. I just thought he was a hot guy working at a dodgy club in town.

I never expected *this* to happen—to see him on Franklin U's campus.

But then again, this is how my life goes. The most ridiculous things happen to me at the most unexpected times.

Like that one time I accidentally entered a hot dog eating contest—and won.

And no, it wasn't the sexy kind of hot dog. It was the kind you put in a bun.

I swallowed those fuckers down like the gay man I am.

I deep-throated those dogs.

Suddenly, the ass I'm staring at turns, and I get a glimpse of the man's face in the daylight. My throat bobs as I take him in. He positively shines. His dark blond hair twinkles in the rays of the sun warming the campus and the shirt he's wearing is glued to his large biceps. He was radiant in the dim, smoky lights of the strip club, practically nude, but here, in the light of day, he's even better looking.

No wonder I came like an animal.

No wonder I spent all last week sitting across the street from that strip club, beating myself up for lurking and yet desperate to go back inside to ask for a repeat.

He's addicting.

"Hey there, Silas. Busy?" someone asks. I jerk slightly, surprised by the interruption and miffed that my ogling has been interrupted. But I can't show anyone this obsession. No, I stuff it down and force a smile on my face. Dr. Brown, the biology department chair and my fellow colleague, looms over me, his graying hair perfectly coifed, his suit and tie immaculate. He's a distinguished professor here on campus, a fan favorite, and I guarantee you he is most certainly *not* coming in his pants from a stripper. Never in his lifetime.

"No, not at all. I was just grading a pop quiz for my Gen Ed Biology class."

"The first week of classes?" he asks with a slightly evil grin.

I snort and bob my head. "You know I like to keep them on their toes."

The truth of the matter is, this isn't some torture technique. It helps me gauge where my students are and where my focus needs to be. It's a way to streamline the learning process for both me and them.

Dr. Brown eyes the stack of papers under my hands and raises an eyebrow. "You know you have a teaching assistant for that, right?"

"I do, but the TA currently hired couldn't start until Thursday, so here I am."

"Ah, I see. Well then, good luck with that. You'll need it."

He winks at me, and I manage another small smile. Dr. Brown is a nice man, just not someone I want to spend too much time with. No, I prefer to spend time alone. Just me and my one-eyed fish named Vertebrata.

Listen, I've never been accused of being unique. I was *this* close to calling her Fish, but the way her eye scowled at me told me she was not impressed.

She's actually quite judgmental and very opinionated.

"Has the semester started out well?" Dr. Brown asks, and I nod.

"So far so good. Had a few students not show up, so I dropped them and then got complaints from them, asking what happened. So, you know, the usual."

"Ah yes, the fun begins. It's the same every year. Never gets old."

I nod and discreetly glance to my left, trying to see if I can get a glimpse of ass-guy again, but I don't see him. He's wandered off. I'll probably never see him again. Which is for the best. I don't need to relive that, nor do I need to entertain ideas of him. I will *not* be driving by or strolling across the parking lot or lurking around the back door of his place of employment now that I'm pretty sure he's a student.

I'm a respectable professor. I don't lust after students. That's never happened in the ten years I've been teaching. And it certainly won't happen now.

Dr. Brown excuses himself after a few more minutes of chatting about the beginning of the semester, and I'm left to sit in the sun, grading the endless papers before me.

I really need to put these assessments online. That would make my life so much easier.

Maybe I'll have my TA help me with that. I do have online course shells where students can log in, check grades, and submit assignments, but I haven't put any of the quizzes or tests online yet. The process of doing so is overwhelming with the office hours I have to keep, the research I need to do, and the committees I am required to serve on. Having a TA enter these online and get it set up would help me greatly.

I make a mental note to ask my TA to do this when I meet him.

Just as I begin to get back to grading, my phone rings. I pick it up, a small laugh leaving my mouth when I see who's calling.

Lee O'Conner.

"Hello, Mr. O'Conner," I say, and I hear shuffling on the other end of the line.

"Silas. It's me. Lee."

I let out a huff of laughter at that. He always does this, announces who he is despite knowing I can see who's calling me. Must be an old habit from the rotary phone days. Lee is ninety-two years old and is honestly the only friend I see on a regular basis.

Even Chris and Gregory are once-a-year friends. Before the abominable dick explosion at the club, the last time I saw them was last spring when they got engaged.

But Lee's different, he makes sure to call me every day just to check in. I think he's lonely but won't admit it. And to be honest, I think I may be as well. My parents were older when they had me, and both passed away years ago. I have a sibling who lives on the other end of the continent, but we rarely speak. Maybe my friendship with Lee reminds me a little of home.

Fuck, I need a change, a fresh start.

Good God, I need to get laid.

"I know who it is. Your name appears on the screen, Lee. I even greeted you by name," I say, leaning back in the wrought iron chair and crossing my legs at the ankles. "What are you up to, old man?"

"Who's calling me old, asshole?" Lee says with a laugh. "I'm young. Mostly."

"Sure you are. So, what are you doing today?"

"Me? Oh, just went on a walk and tried to convince Vera to go on a date with me. She refused."

"I'm sure she did. You're a creep, Lee."

He chuckles at that. "At least I don't send her dick pictures like you do to the guys you're interested in."

I run a hand down my face. "I do not send dick pics to people. Jesus."

"I *know* you do. All the youngins do. My grandson says it's a pandemic with homosexuals these days."

Oh, good lord. I've heard all about his grandson, Junior, the man Lee keeps trying to hook me up with. But I keep refusing. I have no interest in meeting this elusive grandson. We'd probably have nothing in common, and I'd hate to disappoint Lee with any kind of rejection. Who knows how old this Junior is anyways? He's probably just as young as that guy who gave me a lap dance. I already feel like the creepiest of creeps, coming in that chair in that dark, dank club. But dating a man half my age?

No thank you.

I may be lonely and up for a change, but I'm pretty sure that's not it.

"We're gays now, Lee. Homosexual is outdated."

"Meh, I'm too old to change," he tells me, and I roll my eyes with affection.

I met Lee a few months ago while I was shopping at the grocery store. He was slowly wandering the aisles with his walker, and when I noticed that he appeared to be walking back to his place, three grocery bags precariously placed on the little seat, I offered him a ride home.

He told me I was a serial killer and waggled his arthritic finger at me.

I offered to buy him ice cream if he got in the damn car.

He caved like a house of cards.

The rest is history.

I found a fast friend in him that day, and I'm so glad I ended up at that particular grocery store.

"Stop on by tomorrow. I want ice cream and some fries."

"You need to keep your cholesterol under control, old man."

"I may be old, but I'm not dead. Let me live, gay man."

I grin and agree to meet with him tomorrow. Like I'd refuse him. He knows I'm a sucker for spending time with him.

With a quick goodbye, I hang up and get back to work.

The morning wears on, grading taking far too long. Mainly because I get distracted with thoughts of ass-man being a student here and trying to manage the slight anxiety I have at the possibility of running into him and him recognizing me. Perhaps I should purchase a hat and grow my beard out longer.

I should unearth my Groucho glasses and wander the halls with a cane.

A novel idea.

When I finally end up back in my office, only half of the quizzes are graded. *Perhaps I'll leave the rest for the TA to finish,* I think as I open my door for students to come in for office hours. And they do come. The biology classes I teach aren't easy, and I spend a lot of time explaining concepts to students who need it. Perhaps my TA can set up a study group and individual tutoring. Something that will lessen the toll office hours takes on me. Because as much as I do love teaching, interacting with students is draining.

Really, any human interaction makes me want to curl under my desk and hide.

I'm not a real social animal.

Hence the lack of dating. I just can't be bothered.

I do wish a man would literally fall into my lap. It would make everything so much easier.

When I'm finally done with office hours, the last student

ushered out, I shut the door. But before it can close all the way, something stops it, a resistance.

I pull it open, my eyebrows rising at the impertinence of someone trying to stop me from shutting out the world, when I see *him*.

Ass-man. His dark blond hair is swept back from his face, showing me his piercing blue eyes and those pink lips.

And his face. It's even better up close in broad daylight. Flawless, perfect. Absolute sex.

Oh, fuck me.

"Hey, Dr. Sinclair," he says, his eyes scrunching as he smiles at me. A twinkle of something flashes through his eyes, and he bites down on his bottom lip. Oh, he knows. He so fucking knows. My heart rate rises rapidly, and I feel my hands start to sweat. My fingers go up to my tie, and I tug at it, trying to breathe. I can't fucking breathe.

"Sorry I'm late. I'm Everly Winslow. Your TA for your Intro to Biology class."

I let out a very unmanly squeak. "Yes?"

"Yeah. I sent you an email, but you must not have gotten it. I know I was supposed to show up later this week, but I wanted to introduce myself before I just appeared in class."

I shake my head, swallowing loudly. The click resounds around the room, and Everly lets out a huff of laughter. His hand swipes his hair back from his face once more and his bicep bulges as he moves.

Well, good God. He's built.

He could easily pick me up without hurting himself.

I could wrap my legs around his back and ride that cock all while suspended in the air.

His eyes roam down my chest and then pop back up to meet mine, his cheeks flushed, his eyes heated.

Oh. Oh my fuck. This is bad. Very, very bad.

Full Service

"Don't worry. I won't tell. What happens at work, stays at work," he says softly, and I nearly faint from the stress of it all. And partially from horniness. All the blood has left my brain and is currently pooling in my dick.

I'm dizzy from it. Never in my life have I been caught at a strip club, and the one time I get dragged to one and get a lap dance, it's from one of my students. My motherfucking TA.

And I came in my pants.

"Anyways. Enough about that. I brought you coffee from Bean Necessities. Austin makes an awesome cappuccino. I wasn't sure if you like sweet stuff so I went neutral."

I don't know who Austin is, but I accept the disposable cup he offers me. Our fingers brush unnecessarily and my entire body thrums from the contact. I can feel my cheeks heat and watch as Everly's darken.

Oh my god. He likes this as much as I do. He's not even trying to hide it.

I mumble a thank you and take a large sip, burning my throat and tongue in the process.

Great, just great, I think as I sputter and cough. Now I won't be able to swallow for the foreseeable future. Honestly, probably a good thing at this point. It will be a deterrent against falling to my knees and offering to suck his dick.

"Yeah, sorry about that. Told him to make it extra hot just so it wasn't cold by the time I got here. Didn't want to make a bad impression."

He couldn't make a bad impression if he tried at this point. His ass can do no wrong.

"Thank you," I manage to say as I continue to stand in the entrance to my office like an awkward gargoyle. If I perched on a stand I'd look great on some gothic church, I'm sure.

"Um, can I come in?" Everly asks, and I shake my head,

trying to find a reasonable explanation as to why he should absolutely not be in an enclosed space with me.

"I don't think that's a good idea."

He cocks his head at me, some of his blond hair flopping onto his forehead. "Why?"

I don't have an answer. I will deny that it was me in that lap dance chair until I die. I will never admit it. Even though he knows it's me. But a man can lie. And I will use that ability until I'm dead.

"Come on, Dr. Sinclair. It's fine. I really won't tell a soul. It's between you and me."

"I think I'll be taking on another TA," I manage to croak out, feeling a little desperate. I'm having the urge to lie on the floor and hyperventilate. It's a favorite pastime of mine.

His brows rise, and it's his turn to look nervous. "I'd really like to keep this position, Dr. Sinclair. I need it."

The way he says that has me feeling ashamed. I have no idea what he's going through or why he needs this so badly. And truly, it's not his fault I behaved like a feral animal. He was just doing his job. And here I am, trying to fire him on day one.

Well, not even day one. Minus day one.

I'm a scoundrel.

"Fine," I amend and open the door a little further. Everly doesn't even hesitate, just moves into my office, setting his bag down on the ground and taking a seat. He looks good sitting there, that swimmer's back wide at the shoulders and arching down to a narrow waist. I wonder if he swam in high school or even here at the university.

Not that I'm going to try and find out. I would never do that. Probably.

There is a ten percent chance I won't be looking this up.

I move around my desk and settle in my chair, trying not to

look at his thick thighs. They're huge up close, muscular, like he spends his afternoons squatting.

Which he does. On a pole.

I scoot my chair up to the tabletop but move a little too fast and end up knocking into it, making me wheeze.

"Speed racer, huh?" Everly says, and I frown at him, rubbing at my bruised abdomen.

"The rollers on the chair are extra oiled."

"Hm, I do love oiled things."

I stare at him, imagining his oiled chest before reaching for my pen and twirling it in my fingers. I need to do something with my hands so I don't do something inappropriate, like reach across the desk and desperately grab for his crotch.

Or that butt. The one currently in a chair in my office.

It's not my fault that I have some sort of obsession with his ass. He was wearing only a jockstrap that night in the strip club and it was glorious. I've never seen anything like it.

It should be featured in a gallery for all to admire.

My dick gives a precarious twitch, and I give it a very stern mental talking-to. I'll give it a good spanking later.

With my lubed hand.

While *not* thinking of him.

"Anyways, thank you for letting me in," Everly says, biting down on his bottom lip, wetting it in the process. That should absolutely be illegal. I'll have to tell him to never do that in my presence again.

My dick wholeheartedly disagrees.

It wants him to open wide and lean forward.

"I mean, I think you letting me in here means you're not gonna fire me."

I nod, a clipped tilt of my chin and then set my pen down. It clacks noisily on the desktop and I stare at it. It's either that or stare at him.

Why does the most handsome man I've ever met have to be a student here and my fucking TA? Life is laughing at me. Thinks I'm a fucking joke.

I mean, to be fair, it kind of is. A kind of boring joke, but one nonetheless.

"Thanks, man. I mean, Dr. Sinclair. I really promise I can be professional about this."

I nod again and peer up at him, my hands clutching the arms of my chair. The leather squeaks under my sweaty palms. Sounds a bit like an animal whining, like a whimper. Hm, or maybe that's just me.

"That's good. I just want you to know that—"

He raises a hand, interrupting me. "It's fine. You don't need to explain. We can just put it behind us."

That's easy for him to say. He's not a lonely, sex-deprived professor with a hot as fuck TA. I will not be putting any of this behind me. Unless it's my fingers *in* my behind.

"And I'm really good at what I do. I understand biology. I can do whatever you need. Grading, tutoring, study halls. Whatever."

What I need is for him to bend over this desk and pull his cheeks apart so I can see his asshole again, but I digress.

"I'm sure that Dr. Brown chose well. I trust his judgment."

His cheeks flush and he nods enthusiastically. "Of course he did. I didn't mean to imply he didn't know what he was doing. I really respect him."

"And he seems to respect you since you've been hired to assist me."

Everly bobs his head and then a smile splits his face. Fuck, he's even more handsome like this. I must implement a rule that he cannot smile at me. Ever again. He must remain stoic at all times.

"What?" I ask, feeling my heart thunder in my chest.

"I know I said I'd keep it professional, but I just need to say this and I promise I won't say another thing about it."

My jaw clenches as I wait for him to get on with it. He leans forward, the muscles flexing in his arms as he does. My cock positively throbs.

"You just seem so different than you were that night. I like this buttoned-up thing you have going on."

"I was buttoned up just fine that night. I just...lost control for a second."

"Yeah," he says and wets his lips once more. He truly needs to keep that tongue inside his mouth from now on. It's obscene. "And it was brilliant."

"Are you done?" I ask, shifting in my seat and trying to get my boner to go down. It just seems to grow harder.

"Yeah," he replies, leaning back and spreading his thighs open. My gaze flicks down to them before shooting back to his eyes. "Sorry, I just wanted you to know what I thought."

"Well, now we know. Thank you for sharing."

"Anytime. I'm an open book."

I clear my throat, trying to swallow down my lust. It gets stuck in my throat.

"Anyways," I begin, trying to gather my thoughts. He has to be exuding some kind of pheromone that's making me perv like crazy, making me lose the ability to think. I have zero brain cells at the moment. "Dr. Brown has given you my schedule for my classes, and I'll introduce you to them if you have availability. I'm thinking you could set up office hours for students, as well as a study session once a week for those who need it. And I'd like you to grade these pop quizzes and work on getting my assessments online."

He doesn't balk at the list of things I've just asked of him, just pulls his phone out and makes notes.

"Got it. I can do that. When do you need the quizzes back?"

"By Friday. Grades input by then as well."

He nods. "Can do, Dr. Sinclair. I'm a man of many talents."

Our eyes clash, and my heart jumps in my chest. Fuck, he's gorgeous. Good thing I won't need to work closely with him. I'll just put professional distance between us and the lap dance will disappear as if it never happened.

That's my new New Year's resolution. Doesn't matter that it's February and long past the date. I'm a man of my word.

Mostly.

"Alright, well, I'll let you get back to whatever you were doing."

He stands up and my gaze falls to his dick. It's big. I could tell that night, the way it bulged through the fabric. And I can tell now. Those jeans barely contain it. An anaconda.

"Quizzes?" he asks, and I startle at the question. Right. That's what I'm meant to be doing. Without a word, I hand him the stack of papers and the rubric.

"You have access to my course shells?" I manage to ask.

"Yep. IT gave me TA access."

"Good to hear," I say, feeling the need to walk him out but unable to stand up because of my current cock condition. He'll see it. The zipper is barely containing it. Not quite an anaconda, but a nice garden snake.

"You can see yourself out, Mr. Winslow."

He grins at me and leans forward, holding his hand out for me to shake.

I stare at it and bring my sweaty palm up to press against his.

"Nice to meet you. Officially." The way he says that last word sounds like sex.

He's far too tempting, far too much of a lure.

His thumb brushes against the back of my hand and then he releases me, turning around and walking out, leaving me staring after his ass. I even lean across my desk to eye it until it disappears from view, and then I slump in my chair, pressing my forehead against the desk and rolling it back and forth.

I need professional help because this is so out of my wheelhouse.

I don't know how to cope.

* * *

There is a good chance that I may be the most boring person on planet Earth. No one has told me this, but my brain has.

I need a little excitement in my life. Although, any more excitement like the kind I had that night at the strip club can't be good for my heart or my balls.

They exploded. Literally.

I let myself into my small townhouse and set my keys down in the ceramic bowl my niece made for me last year. They clatter and clank as they settle on the bottom of the dish as I toe off my shoes. The suit coat that I purchased from a menswear store hangs on the rack. I remember the young man that helped me fondly. Blaise. He really brought my wardrobe back to life.

I loosen my tie as I walk toward the fish tank and say hello to Vertebrata. She glances at me with her one eye and hides under a piece of coral, a piece of fish poop trailing behind her.

I see how it is.

Don't know why I bothered with her, but then again, I'm a sucker for one-eyed fish.

And peachy asses.

"I know. I can't stand to look at myself either," I say dryly as I place some pellets in the water and move toward the kitchen. The freezer is stocked full of frozen meals, and I grab one, placing it in the microwave, and then pour myself a glass of wine.

Now is not the time to be modest. I give myself a hefty pour, one that nearly sloshes over the edge, and slurp at it as I lean against the counter.

What a day this has been.

A day of realizations.

I sigh and rub at my nose, feeling the beginning of a headache making an appearance. The strain and stress of knowing my TA was the ass-man who made me cum in my pants is almost too much to bear. I was on the verge of panic attacks all day. I hope this anxiety will dissipate the longer we work together, especially now that I know he's not going to tell everyone what happened.

To be fair, the lap dance was the most thrilling thing to ever happen to me. I don't remember the last time I let loose like that.

But then again, I let loose and now the man who helped me accomplish that is a student.

I take another large gulp of wine, feeling my shoulders start to loosen.

Everything will be fine. Everly will behave professionally and so will I.

Even as I think that my dick begins to harden in my pants. To be honest, it was at half-mast all day, but now that I'm alone in my house with no one around to judge me, I feel like perhaps I can loosen up. I can behave in a very disrespectful manner.

Like maybe jacking off to this TA of mine.

It's a bad idea, I think as I squeeze my dick. I can't do this because every time I see him, I'll remember touching myself to the thought of him.

But then again, who will know? Besides me.

My hand slides down the front of my pants, and I clasp the hard, hot length over the fabric.

My head falls back, and I groan lowly. Damn, that feels nice.

Full Service

I take another sip of my wine and feel the rush of alcohol hit my system. The need I've felt all day bubbles to the surface as I set my wine glass down and unbutton the top of my shirt.

Suddenly, the microwave beeps, signaling the meal is done, so I pull my hand away from my pants and grab my dinner, setting it on the counter.

I wash my hands and blow on the steaming food to cool it.

Should probably eat something before I explode all over myself. That's the civilized thing to do.

As soon as the food isn't hot enough to burn, I nearly swallow it whole, washing it down with the rest of the wine before moving to my bedroom.

I have to get off or I may come in my sleep.

And I'll never let myself live that down.

As soon as the door is shut, I strip down to nothing, allowing the cool air to hit my naked skin and pebble my nipples. I pluck at them and gasp at the sensation, my other hand moving down to my dick. It's warm and hard and not deterred at all by what I'm about to do. No, it seems to encourage this deviancy.

Grabbing on to it, I squeeze it and let out a feral grunt.

Oh god, I need this. I have to do this, or I won't survive the semester in his presence. I know I'll regret it once I'm done, but at the moment, it's life or death. If I don't come immediately, I'm going to die.

Reaching into my nightstand, I pull out a dildo and some lube. Usually I'd put on some porn and get off to it, but right now, I don't need it. I have the visual from that night. His bare ass rocking up against my crotch, making me nearly pass out from the sensual image.

I was huffing and puffing the entire time, and Everly Winslow made my cock blow.

Kneeling beside my bed, I stick the dildo onto the ground, the suction cup making a loud squeal as I attach it to the wood floor. With deft fingers, I lube up my hole and then settle back onto the silicone cock, feeling the stretch and burn of it so good as my oiled hand goes to my dick and strokes.

It's slow for a minute until it turns frantic, my ass swallowing the dick behind me as I groan in pleasure.

Everly's face filters through my mind, and I grip my dick harder, jerking it in time with each thrust down.

"Oh fuck yes," I moan as I ride it faster, wishing it was him behind me. Those strong arms bracing me, those thick thighs bracketing mine. That big dick ripping me open.

"Fuck me, fuck me," I grunt, and then without warning, my balls draw up and I explode across my hand and the floor. My body shakes and jerks, my eyes fluttering closed as I picture him —his biceps, his abs, his round, pert ass.

I sit fully on the dildo and let myself experience the sensation of being stuffed full, wishing his cum was painting the inside of me, dripping from my hole.

But reality soon settles in. This is not Everly inside of me. This was all my perverted imagination.

I really am a lonely, creepy fuck.

My hand leaves my dick, and I slump forward, sweating and panting from the exertion. It's then that I feel the shame well up within me. I knew this was going to happen, but did it anyways.

It's going to be a habit now.

I never learn.

I sigh, sliding the dildo from my ass and walking to the bathroom, cleaning up as quickly as I can. My cheeks are flushed, and I wonder if Everly could see my face flame that night as he rocked against me. His eyes were on mine the entire time he faced me, his hips moving rhythmically with the music. And even when he turned around and stuck his ass on my covered cock, he turned his head to watch me over his shoulder.

I never touched. It wasn't allowed, but *he* touched *me*.

It was light, a whisper of movement across the fabric of my shirt, but I felt it.

When I concentrate, I can still feel it sometimes, the drag of his hands across my chest and arms.

I sigh as I wipe up, quickly pulling some casual clothes on before making my way back to the small living room, falling onto the couch and turning on the TV.

I don't really see what show I turn on, my mind on Everly instead.

He's far more fascinating, far more intriguing.

I can't continue to do this. I need to find relief in appropriate places.

Tomorrow, I'll find a solution. I have to. Or I may end up losing my job.

Chapter Two

Everly

"Hey, Austin, how's life?" I greet the guy who works at the coffee cart on campus. His dark copper hair is combed neatly to the side and his freckles seem even more pronounced in the sunlight. How that's possible, I don't even know. But the dude is super cool, quiet and shy as hell but makes an amazing cup of coffee. Probably whispers some kind of magic spell into each cup he makes. I swear, I've never tasted anything like it.

"What book are you reading today?" I ask. I met Austin last fall after I noticed him reading a book on his break. And hell, I do love a good book.

His cheeks flush and he glances down, looking a little embarrassed. "Oh, just the same thing I usually read."

"Yeah, but like what kind?"

This guy. I swear, he reads a book a day. And let me tell you, those romance novels are raunchy as fuck. He lent me one a few months ago from his reading app with a few of the sluttiest lines highlighted, and I read the hell out of it. Couldn't put it down.

Got hard too. Never read about sex like that, and I was there for it. The way the author described dicks...very inventive. And the number of times the guys came was inspiring. I wish I was so virile.

Like Dr. Sinclair. He came untouched.

Is he just super sensitive, or did I make him do that by just existing?

The thought of it is thrilling.

Impressive was one word for it. I had to leave after that dance and jerk off in the bathroom before the next set.

My co-workers knew exactly what I was doing in there too. They mocked me relentlessly.

But I digress, back to romance novels. I'm a sucker for them, even if I don't believe in the concept. I'm not a romantic guy, not like Austin seems to be, given all the swoony lines he highlighted. But I sure do love the smut in some of the books I've read.

Lots of jerk-off fodder.

Like that buttoned-up professor I'm working for, who's totally off-limits, but I can't help but think of when I put my hand down my pants.

"A monster romance, actually."

"Oh yeah? That's cool. Does he have a monster dong?"

"Two actually," he says, and I let out a loud, unexpected laugh.

"Damn, that's one lucky partner he has."

"Yeah. Anyways," he says, his cheeks flushing red. "Same thing you normally get?"

"Yeah, man. Same," I say and then lean forward. "But serious talk now, you got any of the good stuff for me?"

His cheeks darken, and he bites his bottom lip. I sound like I'm asking for drugs and it kind of feels like it too. I have an obsession with smut.

"I do. Let me make your drink, and I can give you the name of one. Wrote it down just for you."

"Awesome," I reply and then move to the other side of the counter to wait. As I do, I watch people in line, captivated by how people behave. Humans are such fascinating creatures.

"Here you go," Austin says, turning my attention back to him. His eyes are lowered as he hands me a piece of paper and the coffee. I clasp both tightly.

"I'll download it and read the fuck out of this," I tell him, and he peeks up at me and grins.

"Enjoy it. Or at least I hope you do."

"I will," I reply before making my way outside.

It's sunny here, even in late winter. That's what I love about Southern California. It's always blue skies, with the occasional rainstorm that sends everyone into a panic. We had one last week and the strip joint closed up shop for the day. I may have spent the entire day jacking off to thoughts of Dr. Sinclair instead of studying.

What a fantastic day that was.

I imagined all the different ways we could fuck each other.

I sling my backpack over my shoulder as I make my way toward class. It's my senior year and I only have one semester left. I transferred to Franklin U my sophomore year and have really enjoyed my time here. But at the same time, I can't fucking wait to be done. Because, while I've enjoyed the experiences I've had, I can't wait to have a degree in something useful so I can quit stripping. Not that I'm not thankful for the opportunities that job's provided me, but I'm just kind of over it.

Unless it's Dr. Sinclair who is sitting in the audience. I'd dance for him any day.

Honestly, you could say I have a little bit of a crush, and have since I saw him on campus last sophomore year. When he showed up at the club, I about died.

I had to fight to be the one writhing on his lap that night.

Speaking of, my eyes pivot to the science center that I'll be working in for the rest of the semester. It's a tall, sleek building with state-of-the-art technology that was built five years ago with a donation from one of the rich alumni who attended the university.

I stop walking and my eyes swivel around the area just out front. And there he is, sitting under a tree on a blanket, his laptop out, his khaki-clad legs stretched out before him. He's wearing a fitted suit and tie, his dark beard neatly trimmed, his hair perfectly combed.

I'd like to run my fingers through it again. Just like I did that night. Mess it up a bit. See him a little mussed and ruffled. I want to lay him down on the blanket and rut against him and watch him gasp as he explodes in his pants.

My dick starts to swell at the thought, and I force my gaze away. I should not go over there and make small talk with him. I definitely should not. I have a class in thirty minutes. I need to focus on my studies and graduating with honors, not flirting with a man who's out of my league.

But despite my internal protests, I make my way over to him, skirting past Jay, another student who happens to be in biology club with me. He's protesting something, wearing a whale shirt and chanting about oil drilling. Fuck me. That's a mood right there. It's the first week of class and these activists have endless energy. I swear these people never sleep.

Although, if I were an activist for something, I'd be a Dr. Sinclair activist, and I wouldn't sleep either.

I'd be too busy trying to activate that man right onto my cock.

Without another thought, I plop down on the blanket right next to him. My presence startles him, and he gasps softly.

"Mr. Winslow," he says, that rough voice making my skin

tingle. He should absolutely not call me Mr. Winslow. It does things to my libido. Actually, Dr. Sinclair does things to my libido just by existing. He is an obsession of mine.

Has been ever since I laid eyes on him. And even more so after he came just from me dancing over his dick.

I've always wanted what I can't have. It's an issue.

"Hi there," I say, my lips pulling up into a smile. My fingers trail across the wool blanket, skirting past his leg. "I just saw you out here, catching some rays, and I wanted to say hello."

"Hello," he mutters and turns his gaze down to his laptop. He's wearing sunglasses, so I can't see where he's looking, but I sure as fuck hope it's at me. I wouldn't mind being ogled by this man. He did it that night, his eyes dark and hooded. Needy.

Lust.

So much lust.

I know it's unprofessional, and I said I'd behave and be professional, but fuck, I sure did like making him come. If he wasn't a professor and technically my boss, I'd give him a private lap dance right now.

But that's off the table.

Dr. Sinclair seems like a rule-following man. I have very little confidence I'd be able to help him break any of them. Seems that night at the club was a bit of a fluke.

But like I said, I always want what I can't have, so it looks like my obsession is settling in for the long haul.

"How are your classes going?" I ask and lean forward, propping my elbows on my knees. He glances at my arms and then at me.

Hm, caught him. Fuck yes.

"Fine."

I take a sip of my coffee, knowing I should leave him in peace, but I can't quite make myself. I want to stay as long as possible and just watch him.

"What are you working on?"

"Answering endless e-mails."

"Ah, yeah, I bet you have a lot coming in since it's the beginning of the semester."

"I do."

I grin at him and his lips twitch slightly.

"So, what does your day look like? I have two classes and then I'm off to work."

He dips his chin slightly, his cheeks turning a little pink. Could be from the sun, or he could be remembering.

He's so remembering. I'm unforgettable.

"Just classes and then back home."

I should not ask, I should close my mouth and let it go, but I can't help myself. "Anyone waiting for you there?"

He cocks his head and shakes it. "Just my fish, who happens to despise me."

A small laugh bursts from me. "Just a fish. No handsome man or beautiful woman?"

"No, and I don't discuss my private life with students."

"Yeah, but I'm technically not your student. I'm your TA."

"Hm. Same thing."

I mean, it's not, but I don't argue. I get where he's coming from, and while part of me doesn't want to push him too much that I end up fired, the other part of me wants to see how far he'll let me go.

He let me go pretty far the other night. All the way actually. I gave him the full service.

"Anyways, how long have you worked here? I transferred from the local community college sophomore year."

He glances down at his laptop and then sighs, closing it.

"I've been working here for about ten years. Was tenured about five years ago."

"Oh, nice. That's a big accomplishment."

Full Service

"It is."

I like watching his mouth move. I want to listen to him talk all damn day, which is something new for me. I usually don't do much talking when I'm around other men.

Do a lot of sucking though.

"Do you like teaching?"

"I like it better than research, but that's part of my teaching requirements so I'm forced to do it."

"Oh shit, yeah, I get that. I mean, I get not wanting to do something but having to." His eyebrows rise at my comment, but I don't explain, not really wanting to make this all about me. "And I actually like research. I'd love to teach a class on research methods or something. One day. Right now, I'm just focused on getting my bachelor's and getting a real job."

"Good plan."

He doesn't ask me any follow-up questions, which is fine. He probably wants me to leave, but I'm not a quitter. And I'm nothing if not determined.

"So, what do you do for fun?" I ask, taking another sip of my coffee. Damn, Austin did real good with this one. He's a wizard, I swear.

"Hang out with my fish," he says dryly, and I let out a laugh.

"Yeah, but besides the fish, man. What do you do?"

"Why do you need to know?"

I shrug. "Just curious."

"Is this some kind of biological research you're doing?" he asks, his lip curling up in a sly grin.

"Oh yeah, totally. This has been approved by the division."

"I'm sure it has," he says, smoothing his blue tie down with his hand. I want to curl my fingers around it and pull him close. Want to grind against his lap and watch as his lips part in desperate pants.

I shift on the blanket and force myself to behave. I can be professional. Mostly. Sometimes.

Never mind. I can't. Not really.

I totally lied to him the other day in his office.

"I don't have many hobbies, I guess. I work a lot."

"I can tell you do, but you have friends, right? I mean, you went to the club with them."

He glances away and runs a hand over his jaw. "Yeah, I do have friends. I see them occasionally. And probably won't again for a while, since they seem to get me into trouble."

"They sure do, and wasn't it fun?"

His gaze flicks back to me and he frowns. "We said we'd keep this professional and not mention that night."

I make a cross over my heart and hold my hand up. "I swear, that was just a slip-up. I won't say another word about it."

I am such a fucking liar.

He crosses his legs, his ankles hooking together. *He has nice shoes,* I think when I glance at the shiny leather loafers he's wearing. I bet those cost a fortune. I glance down at my worn sneakers and make a mental note to get some new kicks soon. Need to impress him in some small way.

"Wanna know what I do for fun?"

"Not particularly."

Those lips twitch again, and I bite back a laugh. This guy.

"Oh, I know you're dying to know. So besides dancing, I love to read. Austin from the coffee shop on campus loans me these romance novels that are super steamy."

"I prefer non-fiction to romance."

"Yeah, but like, have you ever read a romance novel before?"

Dr. Sinclair shrugs. "No. I have no interest."

"Okay, but I'm gonna find a book for you to read and you have to try it."

"Only if you read a historical biography of my choice."

"Sounds boring as fuck, but deal."

Dr. Sinclair clears his throat and then stiffens when a shadow falls over us.

"Hi, Silas, can I speak with you a moment?" a male voice says from behind us. I glance up and see a man with styled brown hair, jeans, and a blazer staring at us. He looks young, not much older than me, and for a moment, I wonder if he's a student here as well.

"Of course. Professor Brooks," Dr. Sinclair says.

Well, shit. This guy is a professor? Damn, I need to graduate and fast. I have some stiff competition here.

Dr. Sinclair turns his gaze back to me, and I get the hint. I need to leave. Not that I want to. I want to stay here and listen to their conversation. Are they going to flirt? Is Dr. Sinclair going to invite Professor Brooks back to his place and show him his fish?

I sure hope not. For some reason, I'm feeling a little possessive over this guy, and I don't even know him, let alone *own* him. And I mean, really, what do I have to offer besides this rockin' bod?

And perhaps a spectacular blow job...and an even better fuck?

In reality, I have a dead-end job, a degree that's not even finished, and a car that's falling apart.

I do have excellent taste in food though and can make a mean artichoke.

I snort to myself as I stand up and throw my backpack over my shoulder. If only I could afford the stuff I actually like to eat.

"Alright, I'll get going. See you later, Dr. Sinclair," I say, and his gaze flashes up to mine for a second before he dips his chin slightly.

So, not even a goodbye then.

That's okay. I'll see him again soon and coax some more conversation from him.

And maybe something more. A touch, a look.

A kiss.

Nah, not gonna happen. I need to nip this little crush I have in the bud and move on.

That's what I'm gonna do. Starting next week.

Or maybe next year.

Hell, maybe when I'm dead.

***

"You look happy today," Mack says, leaning forward in his chair and applying eyeliner under his hazel eyes. He's tall and lean with a stripper's body for days. He was in porn before this job, and I may have watched a few of his videos. For science.

He's a real pro.

Nothing like Silas though.

No, that man gets my obsessive engine going.

"What gives?"

"Just happy to be at work," I say as I throw my stuff into the locker and shut it. It's my Saturday night shift at The Back Door, a strip club that caters to both men and women. Well, mostly men. Although, I have been known to strip for women's night. And let me tell you, the tips are divine. Women really shell out for a good show, and I'm thankful for that.

I need all the help I can get. I refuse to ask my dad for a penny. He's already done too much for me. And my grandpa has no clue how bad it is for me.

I'm on my own. Stubbornly so.

They don't need to worry about me.

"You are not. You're such a fucking liar," Mack says and

then spins in his seat and arches a perfectly shaped brow at me. "We both hate it here and you know it."

"It's not *that* bad. Management could be a little nicer, but it pays the bills."

"Yeah, but you have a chance to get out one day, Mr. Smarty-Pants. You're gonna have a real job in the future. All I have is this. I'm going to die on the stripper pole."

I let out a laugh at his macabre humor. "You quit it. You are not. You're going to find a hot man and have him sweep you off your feet."

"Girl, I will not. I'm not as hot as Julia Roberts, okay? I don't have some rich guy wanting to keep me. And trust me, I need to be kept. I'm far too spoiled for anything else."

"You sure are," I say as I change into my jock strap and then proceed to rub lotion all over my body. Gotta make those muscles pop. When I'm done, I put on my chaps, a vest, and my cowboy boots and get ready to go on stage.

This is gonna be a fun one, I think as I hear the music pumping out in the main room. I can see the lights flickering and the smoke starting to be pumped in from the machine. It's almost time to go put on one hell of a show and my body is prepped and amped up.

Mack stands and winks at me. "You ready, babe?"

"Sure am," I respond as we make our way onto the stage. The cheers and hollers are nearly deafening as we start to dance, our moves coordinated and perfectly in time with the beat. And slowly, we start to strip our clothes off, teasing the audience. They're frantic, the men and women in the audience reaching out for us, wanting to touch, but they're not allowed. Not really. The Back Door might be a little shady, but there are rules.

We kneel to collect the cash they're waving at us, and when my knees hit the stage floor, I feel fingers start to stuff the bills into the waistband of my chaps. Just wait till those come off. We'll make bank.

Which will then go to bills.

To a shitty apartment and marginal food.

But it's fine. I could be doing something else and making minimum wage.

This is more fun and keeps me in shape at the same time. And I'm damn good at it.

I stand up and roll my hips, pulling my chaps off just as Mack does, my eyes moving across the crowd. Bodies, faces, shadows. But in the distance, I see a familiar figure. My heart rate triples, and I find myself losing the ability to breathe from excitement.

My dick twitches and my balls tingle.

He's here.

Dr. Sinclair.

And he's watching me intently.

Chapter Three

Silas

I've made a huge, colossal mistake.

I'm being redundant.

But it doesn't matter. I seem to like making these mistakes. I keep coming back for more.

My back hits the wall in the crowded room, watching as Everly strips his vest off, showing his hard nipples and his oiled six-pack.

Fuck. Me.

My cock twitches in my pants, and I adjust it discreetly, hoping to behave like someone with an ounce of tact and not a screaming, wild animal like the rest of the patrons here.

But then again, I showed up like the creep I am, didn't I?

Everly told me after class yesterday that he had a shift at the club tonight, almost like he was coaxing me, tempting me to show up.

"I work Saturday, just so you know. At ten."

I pretended like I didn't hear it, like it was just white noise in my ears, but I did. I etched the info into my mind. I even went online when I got home to double-check that he was, in fact, working. And there he was, in all his half-naked glory on my computer screen, beckoning me.

I was doomed from the beginning. I should just lie down and accept my fate.

The crowd cheers, and a woman tries to crawl onto the stage, immediately being pulled back by a large bouncer with a head bigger than my torso. She's behaving how I feel deep down —a clawing, feral thing.

But then again, Everly knows how to work a crowd. His co-worker up on stage isn't half bad either. They put on a good show together, and yet I can't tear my eyes away from *him*.

From the way his muscles shine under the lights, the way they bunch and move, the cocky smile he wears on his face as he undulates his hips.

Fuck me. What kind of word is undulate? I need to get a grip. I should walk out of here immediately because this is completely inappropriate. I shouldn't be here watching my TA strip off his clothes and stick his ass out to the world.

And yet, here I am.

With a leaking boner.

The ground must be extra sticky from bodily fluids and alcohol because I cannot get my feet to move. I might have to spend the night here, propped up against the wall, pretending to blend into it. I could probably manage it too. I'm wearing a dark button-up shirt and black slacks. If I don't move and I close my eyes maybe no one will be able to see me. I'll become one with the wall. Just a bodyless face.

I glance back up at the stage and my eyes connect with Everly's.

My breath catches, and I feel my skin break out in goosebumps.

Oh shit. I've been caught.

He's seen me.

Maybe I can slink away and deny this until the day I die. But the way he's watching me, there's no point in even attempting this. His gaze is locked with mine. The way he's moving his body, his hands on his chest and then clutching his groin.

Every move feels like it's for me.

I know it is.

I can see the way he bites his lip, how he wets his mouth. And when he pulls his pants off and flaunts his ass to the crowd, I know that he's showing me what I've been missing. His head keeps tilting back over his shoulder, glancing in my direction. And I keep staring at him, unable to breathe.

He likes that I'm watching, that I'm debating what I could do to that body of his if I had fewer scruples.

But then again, scruples?

Seems I don't have any.

Don't even really know the word.

It's not in my dictionary.

And if I look but don't touch, that doesn't count, right?

That's how I got myself to come here tonight. It's just a show, simple entertainment on a Saturday night. Nothing more. It's not like I'm going to let him touch me, let him get me off again. Not that he needed to touch me to do that.

I reach down and squeeze my dick. It positively throbs, an ache that goes straight down my legs and makes them shake. I'm close and he's done nothing but writhe on stage.

Imagine if he was naked on top of me...

I'd embarrass myself. I'd put the gays to shame with how fast I'd come.

Shitty Stamina Silas Sinclair.

I should get a jersey with that name on it. Wear it on my nights out so everyone knows to stay away.

I'll make it red too.

Red flag!

"God," I murmur as the back of my head thunks on the wall, my dick doing all sorts of inappropriate things. It's currently waving at Everly and trying to entice him with a wink. And who could blame it? Look at him.

Fucking look at him.

I groan softly at the way he rolls his hips, the way his abs flex into six perfect squares, his hands behind his head as he watches me. No wonder I lost control when I was getting that lap dance. He's all-consuming. I can feel him in my balls, tingling, drawing me close to release just from looking at me.

He's sex personified.

I reach down once more, trying to tame my dick into submission, but my palm ends up rubbing against my length instead. I'm basically masturbating in public at this point, and I don't even care if anyone is looking. Not that they are. Their eyes are focused on the men on stage.

Oh fuck, oh fuck.

I want to stick my hand down my pants and jerk it, to give it some relief, but I don't know if I need to. This may be enough, this friction of my palm digging into my dick.

Everly turns around and leans forward, his ass on display once more and he does some flick with his waist that has his cheeks bouncing. I squeeze the base of my dick as hard as I can, to hinder any kind of pre-ejaculation, but I just can't manage to stave it off. The visual before me is too much, too enticing, and without warning, my cock erupts in my pants. I gasp and groan at the sensation, my boxers flooding with cum.

Oh, hell no. I came barely touched, just from the sight of him.

I twitch and shiver, riding it out as long as I can. And as soon as it's done, shame washes over me and I feel my cheeks heat. Oh my god, what the hell am I doing? What the hell is this?

I need to leave. I need to escape before he sees me. One glance down at the wet patch on the front of my pants will tell him all he needs to know.

He managed to make me come. Again.

And this time, all he did was stand there flexing the globes of his ass.

I punch my leg to get my feet unstuck from the ground and then I'm off, nearly jogging across the parking lot, my coat flapping behind me, my release dripping down my legs. My dick is rapidly softening and feels none of the shame I currently do.

I am a thirty-five-year-old tenured professor. I should not be behaving this way.

Foolish, is what this is. Unhinged.

I scramble to my car and just as my hand hits the handle and a beep signals it's unlocked, I hear my name called out from across the dimly lit lot.

I am going to get murdered and they're gonna find me with underwear full of splooge.

"Dr. Sinclair!" the voice calls out again.

A wince takes over my face. Oh god, don't out me. For fuck's sake.

I turn slowly, trying to behave naturally, but there he is, shivering in his small jock strap and cowboy boots. He looks positively edible.

"Jesus, Everly," I say and then clear my throat, peeling my jacket off and handing it to him. When he doesn't take it, I place it around his bare shoulders and hold it closed. His eyes are shining when I finally meet his gaze.

"You're leaving?" he asks, and I nod, feeling so ashamed.

"I didn't realize you'd be performing tonight," I lie. "It's inappropriate that I was here, to say the least."

He rolls his lips between his teeth and nods. "Did you not enjoy the show?"

My eyes fall to the side. I did enjoy the show and that's part of the problem.

"You are very good at what you do," I say diplomatically. It's the least I can do when I behaved so abominably mere minutes ago.

"Good. I'm glad you liked it. But will you wait for me, so I can see you after I'm finished?"

I shake my head, feeling my dick try and perk up in my pants despite having just released a minute ago. It's ready for more action.

"I really need to get home. This was a mistake."

Everly's mouth turns down, and he takes a step back. "Yeah. Of course. I'll just go. I'm sorry you were disappointed."

He looks so forlorn that I stop him with a hand to his arm.

"Wait, it's not...it's not you. It's me. I shouldn't have come tonight."

Everly's eyelids flutter. "But I liked dancing for you."

A small whimper escapes me, and I feel my body grow tense. "It was wrong of me to show up here."

"I don't mind. I really don't. I like that you liked it, that you like watching me."

"I do," I admit and then shake my head. "But nevertheless, I need to go. Home. To my fish."

His chin meets his chest and then he peers up at me. "Okay. But just know that I'm glad you came tonight." He hands me back my coat and then turns to head back inside.

I want to tell him that I'm glad I came too, but that would be a lie. I'm not glad. I feel like a fool and worry that this is going to affect our working relationship.

That he's going to tease me relentlessly with that smile, with that ass, and I won't be able to live it down. So I just watch him go in silence.

But when Monday rolls around, he acts like none of it ever happened. Like I didn't cream my pants watching him dance on stage. Like I wasn't ogling him and behaving like a pervert.

"Hey, Dr. Sinclair," he says softly as he enters my office. It's the start of my office hours, and I'm feeling like I spent the weekend drinking. Not that I did. No, I spent my time ruminating on the fact that I've turned into some kind of stalker creep.

And I also spent an inordinate amount of time jacking off in my room. I did not do it in the living room where Vertebrata could see. She'd shame me, I'm sure.

She has standards and I'm not up to par.

"I brought you a coffee. A toffee nut latte actually."

"You don't need to buy me coffee."

"I know, but I like it, bringing you little presents."

That is completely inappropriate and I should reject the offer, but the drink does sound lovely and I'm nothing if not a pushover.

I take the cup from him and stare at the opening, worried that if I glug it down I'll burn my tongue again. But he shakes his head and explains, "It's not too hot. I knew I'd make it here on time so I got it a normal temp."

My lips curl around the opening, and I take a small sip, letting my eyes close at the taste of sugar this early in the morning. It's glorious. I don't usually let myself indulge like this.

"This is detrimental to my body, just so you know. I can't drink stuff like this and look the way you do."

His eyes slash to my chest and then back up to my gaze. "You look just fine to me."

I don't move a muscle, not wanting to encourage this, any of it. I need to *behave*.

There's an eight percent chance I'll behave.

"I mean, you're a bit older than me..." His words trail off. "How old are you, by the way, Dr. Sinclair?"

"Too old for you," I say, and he lets out a small laugh.

"Nah, I don't believe in that shit. No one is too old for another. Unless it's like creepy pedo shit, then that's nasty."

I arch an eyebrow at him, and he leans forward.

"So, come on. Tell me. I'm twenty-one. How old are you?"

I should not engage, and yet my mouth decides otherwise. "Thirty-five. Almost thirty-six."

He bites the corner of his lip and his eyes sparkle, like the blue of the Pacific Ocean in the summer. Blue and glistening. I could get lost in there, just drown in their depths.

"That's a good age. Thirty-five."

"Almost thirty-six, and this is not something we should be discussing."

He clears his throat and sits back, his eyes slipping from me, and I feel the loss of his gaze palpably.

"I didn't say anything wrong," he says, a little too confidently. And truth be told, he didn't, not really, but the innuendo was there. He thinks that thirty-five is a good age for *him*. But I know something he doesn't. It's most definitely not.

I have almost fifteen years on him. A lot can happen in that time.

The truth of the matter is, we have nothing in common. Besides biology and my newfound love of strip clubs.

"I have office hours now," I tell him, and he nods in understanding.

"Yeah, I get that. That's why I'm here. To help out. This is why you have a TA, right? To lessen your workload?"

"Correct," I say as I take another sip of my coffee. Damn, this's good. It's something I'd never get for myself, and yet I find my eyes nearly rolling back in my head from the sugary sweetness of it. Today I'm letting myself enjoy the treat.

My usual cup of black coffee can wait until tomorrow.

"Well then, let me help you, Dr. Sinclair."

The way he says my name, the way it rolls off his tongue, makes my dick perk up in my pants.

Good fuck, I need therapy.

Dick therapy.

"Fine, you can use the desk in the corner and we can split up students if we need to. Sometimes I have a line a mile long."

He nods and then moves to his spot in the office, setting his backpack down and pulling out an iPad. Within minutes, students start to appear, and just like he said, he helps to mediate the rush of them. I find my eyes straying to him when students are speaking to me, watching the intent way he leans forward and listens to what they're saying, how easy it seems to be for him to interact with them, and how well he explains concepts.

I wish I'd had that ability early on. There are still times where I want to pull my hair out in frustration trying to explain concepts that are so easy to me and yet students struggle with. But I'm paid too well to do that. Plus, I happen to quite like that I still have all my hair. It's my best feature at this age.

When my office hours end a few hours later, Everly stands up and stretches, his shirt riding up a bit and showing off the smooth tan skin beneath. I saw that skin the other night, watched it ripple in the lights of the stage, and came in my pants like a rascal.

I need to stay away from him. He's far too dangerous. In so many ways.

"Alright, I need to get to class. Biostatistics," he tells me.

I force my gaze to move away from his sexy abdomen. I will speak to his face, I will make eye contact.

"Ah yes, such fun."

He grins at me, those white teeth flashing. "Yeah, it kinda is. I'm a nerd like that. Anyways, see you tomorrow, Dr. Sinclair."

And with that, he turns on his heel and disappears from view, and I'm left to sit in my chair and try to fucking control myself.

"You will behave like a gentleman," I tell my dick.

It just hardens from the reprimand.

I'm fucking hopeless.

* * *

My dick does not behave.

Of course it doesn't. I'm walked all over. I'm unable to stand my ground.

I'm lingering behind the podium in the Intro to Biology lecture hall, going through my slides for my presentation when Everly walks in.

Heads turn, watching as he makes his way down the aisle, a bag slung carelessly over his broad shoulders, his tight gray shirt accentuating his muscles, those jeans clinging desperately to his thick thighs.

My dick instantly takes notice and lifts its head, straining toward him. It's an unseemly bulge at the worst of times. I really need to get him under control.

My dick. Not Everly.

He needs to stop being so sexy.

"Fuck," I murmur, hoping that no one is looking at me and reading my lips. It's so unprofessional, swearing at work. And yet, I can't help myself. I have a boner in a class with at least two hundred students seated before me. There's no way I can move away from this podium while he's here. Everyone will see it. Damn these tight dress pants that Blaise told me I should buy. I really need to take to wearing those baggy jeans they wore in the nineties. At least I could hide my unruly dick.

"Hey, Dr. Sinclair," Everly says softly and grins at me.

I adjust my tie and force my eyes to move back to my laptop. If I start drooling, there's no telling what people will think. Perhaps they'll think the best and assume I have a salivary gland issue. At worst, they'll know I'm drooling over my TA. Which is completely inappropriate.

"Mr. Winslow. I take it you're here to introduce yourself and let them know about your office hours and study group?"

"Yep, here to offer the full service to them."

That makes me peer over at him. "Is that so?"

His grin widens. "Yup. You know how multifaceted I am. A man of many talents."

I do. I've seen what he can do with those hips.

I'd like to see what he could do with his tongue and that dick.

"Right, then go ahead and get class started, and when you're done, I'll take over."

Everly nods and when everyone settles in their chairs, he takes the microphone from me, holds it up to his mouth, and begins to speak.

I watch as he does this, alternating between ogling him and pretending to look at my laptop. But it's hard to look away from him. The way he speaks, so confidently, so assured.

I wish I'd been like that in my early twenties. It was only a few years ago that I started to really believe in myself. And there are days when I still don't know what the fuck I'm doing.

Like right now.

Why the hell am I getting a boner over this guy? He's far too young for me and my TA on top of it. I'm behaving like a wayward teenager.

And yet, my mind knows why. It's so simple.

He's hot as fuck.

And I'm a lonely, sad man.

"If you have any questions, you can email me, or here's my number," he finishes.

I frown when I see multiple students start scribbling his number down. I would too if I were them. I'd be messaging him at all hours if I were fifteen years younger. Probably would send him pictures of my dick and butthole too.

"You can jot that down, if you want," Everly says softly to me, and I feel my cheeks heat. "Just in case you have a biological emergency and need assistance."

He glances down at my crotch, and I shift my hips away from him.

I clear my throat and adjust my jacket. "Thank you for coming in today, Mr. Winslow. I'm sure you have a class to get to."

He nods, his lips twitching with mirth. "I do. So I'll see you around."

I dismiss him with a nod of my head, and if my hand inadvertently writes down his number when he's gone, it's not my fault. I may need him at some point.

In a very non-sexual, very platonic way.

My dick does not control me.

I am my own man, thank you very much.

* * *

I used to have a nightly ritual of coming home, microwaving a meal, and falling into bed with a good biopic about some long-dead person.

I have no clue why I'm still single. I'm such fun. A true catch.

But now, things have changed. I haven't gone back inside

the club to watch Everly dance because that ended terribly, and I honestly can't stomach the thought of coming in my pants again. I don't think I could live down the humiliation. And I don't want to end up like some kind of stalker featured on a television show a year from now. It was bad enough that Everly saw me cream myself the first time and caught me in the club the second time around. I will not crawl my way into the shoddy little strip club and get off to the sight of him again.

But I have made it a bit of a habit to walk by the club each night after eating dinner. It's just for the exercise, I tell myself. I'm getting up there in age and The Back Door is close enough. I should really get a dog so I can have the excuse that I need to walk him. Perhaps Vertebrata would enjoy a nice stroll around town.

I should buy some kind of portable fish bowl and take her out. I bet she'd like that. She's a real social animal. She can scowl at passersby.

I scoff as my footsteps slow outside the club. The bouncer outside waves at me, and I feel my cheeks heat. He obviously knows me by now. I've been by here the past four days. Like clockwork.

"How you doing, boss?" the man calls out.

I should really find out what his name is. It would only be polite.

I straighten my shirt and lift a hand in response. "Good, you?"

"Good, man. Nice night. Could rain later though. Better get back before it does."

"Yeah, I will."

"Your boy's working tonight, just so you know."

I nod, feeling my cheeks flame to epic proportions. I didn't come by knowing when Everly was working. I forced myself not to look. And it doesn't matter anyways. I'm not going inside.

Not now and not ever. I've already crossed too many lines with him. So many lines that have been obliterated and crushed into dust.

And yet, here I am once more, a glutton for punishment, it seems.

I force my gaze away from the club and continue walking. I need to get a grip, need to behave like a grown man. This is slightly unhinged and most definitely unhealthy, and yet I can't quite let it slide. I can't quite let him go.

I walk past a few businesses on my trip home. As I glance in the window of Indelible Ink, I wonder if I should get a few more tattoos added to the ones I already have on my forearm. The little biology symbols, my mom's favorite book, my dad's favorite quote. Although, perhaps not. It's time to grow up and behave like an adult.

A feat I'm not succeeding at right now.

Perhaps it's been too long since I've had someone to come home to, had someone who took an interest in me, or maybe it's simpler and more base than that. Maybe I just need to get fucked.

And fucked good.

The first raindrop hits me as I make my way down a residential street a few blocks from my townhouse. By the time I arrive home, I'm nearly drenched, my hair dripping water into my eyes.

"Well, fuck," I say as I enter my place and strip my shirt off. Vertebrata is staring at me through the glass of her fish tank, but when I move toward her, she swims away and hides in her small coral cove.

If I didn't know any better, I'd think she hates me.

Maybe she needs a friend too. I should buy her another fish to spend time with.

Full Service

I peel myself out of my pants and walk to the bathroom where I shower and throw on some sweatpants.

I should just call it a night and go to sleep. But instead, I find myself on my bed with my laptop, pulling up the strip club website, just to get a glimpse of Everly on the front page. It's just a photo of him stretched out against a pole, oiled up and positively muscular. I pull my dick out of my pants and jack myself to the thought of him.

It's become a nightly ritual. Edging myself by walking by the club and then coming home and getting myself off to the mere thought of him. I've moved past sad and am in just plain depressing territory.

When I'm done, I mop up my cum and lean my head back and sigh.

"I really need to get a life," I say just as my phone rings.

I scramble to grab it and grin when I see who it is.

"Hey, Lee," I say.

"Hi, Silas. This is Lee."

I roll my eyes and walk out of my room, leaving the stench of cum where it belongs. It definitely does not need to be a part of this conversation.

"What's up, Lee? You okay?"

"Yep, as good as a dying man can get. But you know what I'd really like? Some fries."

My eyebrows rise. "Is that so?"

"Yes. The really good chili fries that they have at that Food Cafe place."

"They're closed right now. It's late. Way past your bedtime."

He sighs. "You need to help out an old man, Silas. I may not be alive tomorrow. This is my last wish."

I scoff at that. "You're healthier than me. Quit it. But fine, I'll take you to a diner that's open. And we'll get you those fries you can't live without."

"There's my boy."

It warms my heart to hear him call me that. It's been so long since my parents died. The only family I have left are my sister and my niece who live in Florida. Might as well be on another continent for as often as I see them. Or hear from them. I get that it's a two-way street, but I honestly can't be bothered.

Seems I'm doomed.

"You ready to go now?"

"Yep. I even have my shoes on."

"Good man. I'll be there in fifteen."

"I'll wait outside."

With a flick of my finger, the call is ended and I'm on my way out to my car to pick him up. He lives in a retirement home about ten minutes from me, and after he slides into my car and I stick his walker in the trunk, a quick Google search lands us at an all-night diner with food that will put us both in an early grave.

"Can't believe you're still awake," I tell him.

"Gotta be to keep up with you youngins," he says as he takes a big bite of his chili fries. I did try to persuade him not to order this because he's going to regret it later. I don't think his stomach can cope, or his bowels, but he just glowered at me until I caved.

"Plus my son and grandson are busy people. I have to stay up late so I can chat with them. If I didn't, I'd never speak to them. Same with you."

"Lies. I visit you at least twice a week and bring you lunch."

"True, but then you're running off to your next thing. When do you have time to relax?"

"Never. I have to work to afford life in California. Not all people can be Boomers with hefty retirement funds and stocks from the 1950s."

He chuckles at that and then holds up a chili-soaked fry to me. "You're a little shit. Come on, eat up, sad man. And tell me how you're going to enjoy life from now on. And don't lie. You need to tell me the truth. I have to live vicariously through you."

"Fine. I'll go on more walks," I tell him but leave out the incriminating *past the strip club* to make myself seem a little less creepy. "And maybe I'll even get a new tattoo."

Lee's eyebrows rise. "Is that so? Of what?"

"I have no idea."

"Seems you need to get out more and find something that inspires you."

The only thing that seems to inspire me is Everly and his butt. But it's not like I can tell Lee that. He'd never let me live it down. He's a bit of a perverted old man when it comes to stuff like that. One time he told me I should snowball men more.

I don't think he knew what snowballing meant. But then again, I just don't know. The way he grinned at me told me he may have figured out how to work his phone and looked it up.

We chat some more as I sip on some tea. Lee finishes off his fries, lifting the paper underneath them and licking it clean, like a raccoon. Some paper peels off into his mouth and he actually swallows it. Jesus. But then again, who cares? I used to feel slightly embarrassed by the display he puts on when he does things like this, but now I just shrug it off.

Makes him happy. Who am I to judge?

At least Lee doesn't lurk outside of a strip club and lightly stalk a student.

When it comes to creepy, I'm winning.

I should come with a warning sign.

After I drop him off, I tell myself to go home. Straight home. Crawl into bed and read a book, but my car drives me right to the strip club, and I find my eyes settled on the back entrance of the club, wishing that Everly would just stride out and take all choice away from me by sucking my dick into his mouth.

But of course, that's the dream of a crazy person. It obviously doesn't happen, but the urge to enter the establishment and lurk is making my skin itch.

I really should just go in. Sneak in and watch, see if he's even performing tonight.

Fuck me. I'm lying to myself now. I know he's on stage. I checked. I check every night. It's a ritual.

Get home. Microwave dinner. Check if Everly's working. Jerk off.

And now I've apparently added another thing to my schedule.

Stalking.

I'm a man of many talents.

I lean my forehead against the steering wheel and groan, my hand going between my legs and squeezing my dick. I will not get off here. I just did that at home. Somehow doing it in a dimly lit parking lot seems a lot more unhinged.

So I don't. I *will not*.

Suddenly, a loud bang has me lifting my head up, and I see Everly stride out of the club, wearing a silk robe, his phone held up to his ear. He laughs loudly, a sound so endearing that I find myself shivering as I peek over my dashboard at him.

I should leave, but I'm worried he'll notice if my headlights flick on.

So I just sit there, my hand on my crotch, my eyes blinking wildly as I watch him. He's leaning up against the brick building and chatting happily. He hasn't noticed me, thank fuck, because I really can't explain this away.

But then my luck runs out. His eyes flick across the parking lot, and I see him freeze. Fuck. He's seen me. I know it. Trying to scoot down as far as I can, I accidentally honk the horn with my arm and groan.

Way to *not* draw attention to myself. I try to sit down on the floor but end up stuck halfway between the steering wheel and the seat. My leg starts to cramp from the awkward way I'm sitting, and I realize that in the process of trying to hide, I turned the blinker on and the windshield wipers.

Seems I'm turning left in the rain at the moment, huffing a small laugh because it's either that or cry.

Knock. Knock.

The tap on my window has me looking up bashfully.

And there he is, grinning down at me.

"Kill me now," I murmur, trying to sit up but realizing I really am stuck. If he calls the fire department, I will run away and never come home again.

But mercifully, he doesn't call for help. Instead, he opens the door and pushes the seat back as far as it can go, letting me extend my legs and clamber out of the car. As I do, I fall forward and his strong arms engulf me.

This is the closest I've ever been to him, besides the night of the lap dance. But this time my hands are on his strong chest and my face is smashed into his shoulder. I can smell the sweat of his skin, feel the frantic way he's breathing.

It's overpowering.

A drug.

"Easy there, Dr. Sinclair."

I wince and pull away, feeling suddenly ashamed. I've never behaved so dreadfully.

"Thank you. I had a bit of a mishap."

"Seems you did," he replies, placing his hands in his robe pockets and cocking his head at me.

I run a hand down my chest and glance away from him, trying to regain my composure. Seems there's none to be found.

"Would you like to come inside?" he asks, and I say no far too quickly. Even I don't believe myself.

"You'd prefer just to stay outside?" he asks, biting down on his bottom lip, trying to contain a grin. "I mean, the view is better inside."

"Pfft. I know that." I run a hand through my hair and sigh. "But, really, I need to go home. I have an early meeting tomorrow."

He takes a step toward me, and I stagger back, needing to keep my distance.

"Are you sure? I could give you another lap dance. On the house."

The way his eyes twinkle makes my heart throb. And by heart, I mean dick.

"That is a terrible way to do business, Mr. Winslow. You should never give anything away for free."

He grins at me, showing me those perfectly white teeth. "Yeah, but I can if I want to. So, do you want to come in and let me show you some of my new moves? I have a new routine, one I created just for you."

"Absolutely not."

"Why? Is it because it's unprofessional?"

"Yes. It is."

"So is walking past the club every night."

I gasp and glower at him. "I do not."

He reaches out and gently touches my chest. It's just his finger, but it makes me lose my ability to breathe. I need a lung transplant. I have some kind of breathing condition.

"Bruce told me."

"Bruce is wrong."

"Nah, he has eyes like a hawk. Says you come by like clockwork every night."

If my face gets any hotter, my cheeks are going to melt off. A puddle on the floor. Who needs them anyways? The ground can have them. Stupid things.

He fiddles with the tie of his robe, and my eyes lock onto it.

"Come on in, Dr. Sinclair. No one needs to know. Just between you and me. Our secret."

But I'll know. I'll know, and I will feel like shit about it.

I think.

There's a four percent chance I'll feel bad about it.

"I have a private room ready for us."

Well, that's entirely too tempting.

"I refuse," I say, even though my dick is disagreeing. It completely accepts the offer. We should go in, sit in that private room, and let Everly rub all over us.

Make us come our eyeballs out.

"Yeah, no pressure," he says as he pulls his robe open and shows me the jockstrap he's wearing. My mouth drops open and only closes when he reaches out, his fingers pressed under my chin, snapping my jaw shut.

"Take a good look, Professor. See what you're refusing."

He turns around and lifts the robe far too sensually and shows me *that ass*.

Well, shit.

And then he's sauntering off, like a goddamn king, and I'm left staring after him.

I will not go in.

I cannot.

Chapter Four

Silas

Last night was my Mt. Everest. I climbed and I conquered. I didn't go into the club and have my TA rub all over my cock.

I just went home and jerked one off in the shower like the winner I am.

And then again this morning when I woke up.

And then again before I left for work.

I've increased my stamina. I have a nice refractory period now.

But this is not my fault. Everly is going to be within touching distance today. So, the masturbation sessions were necessary. I need all the help I can get. And by help, I mean draining my balls to the point where they're shriveled like figs.

If I go to the bathroom halfway through office hours and fuck my fist, well, there's only so much I can do about it. My libido has taken over my life.

Everly is potent.

"Hey," he says, appearing in the doorway of my office and

looking fucking delicious. He's wearing a t-shirt that's so thin it's nearly see-through and tight pants that show off every muscle in his legs...and the outline of his dick .

He knows what he's doing.

He knows how vulnerable I am. He's basically a predator right now. And I'm his prey.

The door clicks shut behind him and he leans forward, setting a cup of coffee on the desk in front of me.

"Trying to gain favor? Sucking up?" I ask with a raised eyebrow. I'm playing it cool. I am as cool as a cucumber.

"Not *quite* the thing I'd like to suck, but yes. In a way."

I nearly choke at his response and shift in my seat. My office hours start in twenty minutes, and I know that we're playing a dangerous game. Anyone could walk in and see this. Hear it.

It becomes even more detrimental when he sets his bag down and instead of just dropping it like a normal person, he bends down at the waist, pushing his ass out and moves it up and down slowly.

I stare at it, motionless. It's perfectly round. I want to stick my dick in it.

He stands up an inch at a time and then prowls toward me. If he crawls across my desk, I'll lose my shit.

I will drop my pants and beg for it.

But he doesn't do that, he just moves to stand near me and squats down. But not a normal squat. A sensual one, where his crotch calls to me. A mating call.

He knows what he's doing.

"You are ridiculous," I grunt, and he grins up at me, those beautiful blue eyes watching me so intently.

"Just showing you what you missed out on last night, Dr. Sinclair."

My cheeks turn red, and I should look away, but I can't. I just ogle him, unblinking. My eyeballs start to dry out, and I worry, for a moment, that they might shrivel up like raisins. Might be a good thing. Then I won't lust after Everly anymore.

His hand reaches out and he spins my chair to the left, forcing me to face him. I really should get a seat without a swivel. This is a hazard.

When I'm facing him, my thighs parted, he scoots closer to me before standing up, slowly, his groin doing miraculous things. I swear. I've never seen someone so hot before in my entire life. His crotch is hypnotic.

His hands land on the back of my chair, and he straddles my legs, undulating his hips and making me whimper.

This is ridiculous. I should push him away. But I don't touch him. I only hold on to the chair tighter, trying to get my pulse under control. It doesn't work. The way he's moving his hips is only making my blood pressure rise, and I feel lightheaded.

If I come in my pants and have to sit in my mess all through my office hours, I'm going to fire him.

"Drink your coffee, Dr. Sinclair," he whispers, his mouth brushing my ear as he slowly moves away from me, leaving me wheezing. I can't breathe. Every atom that keeps me together, every coherent thought is currently residing in my dick. My balls aren't so shriveled anymore. They're hard and aching.

He huffs a small laugh as he turns me around, his hands clasped onto my shoulders. And then he's gone, putting a respectable distance between us. And I still can't cope.

I'm trembling.

He doesn't seem to notice though. He just plops down at the other end of the office and drags his bag over to him, bending over like a normal person for the first time since entering my space, and pulls his iPad out.

I stare at him, wondering if I imagined the entire thing. But I can still feel his hands on my shoulders, his lips on my ear, and I know that there's no way I could make that up.

He was giving me a taste of what I missed out on.

But he really doesn't need to rub it in. I already fucking know.

* * *

As soon as office hours end, I breathe a sigh of relief. It means that Everly will leave and I can sit in peace and panic.

My dick did go down thankfully, but now that the last student has left, it perks back up. It's relentless. It's becoming a bit of a problem.

Everly stands up, stretches, and then closes the door. The click resounds around the room, and I force myself to look away from him.

"That went well, I think," he says, rustling around in his bag. I hear the crinkle of paper but that's all I know.

I won't look. I won't. If he does another stripper move, I will just explode all over myself. There will be no stopping it.

"Want a candy?" he asks, and I nod because I can't open my mouth to refuse. It's stuck in place and can't form words.

He moves toward me and holds a hard round orb out to me. Something I've never heard of, I'm sure. It's bright pink, and I wonder for a second what flavor it is. I hope it's not watermelon.

Fucking hate that shit. Water should not be in a melon. It's unnatural.

"Open," he says, and I peer up at him. He looks mischievous but my mouth still splits apart and his fingers press the candy gently inside. The first thing I notice is that his fingers are in my mouth and my tongue curiously peeks out and slides against those rough pads.

He lets out a shaky breath and our eyes lock.

Right before I scrunch up my face in disgust. Fucking melon water.

"Shit, you don't like that flavor? How about lemon?" he asks, leaning down. "We can trade."

He holds his tongue out and a yellow candy sits there. An invitation.

"Come on. Open up, Dr. Sinclair," he says, his mouth now inches from mine.

I should not. I absolutely should not. Anyone could walk right in and see this erotic display. And yet, my lips widen and he tilts his mouth over mine, his tongue swiping against mine and swapping the candies like a pro.

Probably some kind of hot drug dealer. Probably does this with all his clients.

If I was one, I'd pay money for the feel of his tongue in my mouth.

"There," he says, pulling away, his lips slightly wet.

My spit is on them. I can taste him in me.

Oh good fuck, I'm a goner.

"Better?"

I just let out a little croak.

He grins widely. "Love the little noises you make. They really turn me on."

He reaches down and adjusts himself, bringing my eyes to his crotch. What would that big dick stretching me out feel like?

I will never find out.

There's a nine-point-five percent chance that won't happen, that I'll resist any future advances.

"What are you doing now?" he asks, and I stare at him.

I will not tell him that I plan on grabbing dinner.

"Dinner," I say, and he sighs, running a hand through his hair.

"Awesome. I'm hungry too. Let's go grab something to eat."

"That wasn't an invitation," I say as my teeth crack down on the lemon candy in my mouth.

"Yeah, it was. You know it. I know it. Come on. Let's go to the Food Cafe."

"That's expensive."

"Yeah, but, Dr. Sinclair, you can afford it. You're a tenured professor."

My cheeks heat at that, the confident way he flirts with me. It's so inappropriate.

"But real talk. Let's go because if you keep sitting there..." He blows out a breath and my dick leaks in response. "Just...we need to go."

I stand up and adjust my dick. I've given up on Everly not seeing it. He knows what he does to me. He's taunting me by simply existing. To say I have a crush on this man would be trivial. It's more than that.

It's an obsession.

Grabbing my satchel, I move out of my office, locking it behind us and walking with Everly as we make our way off campus. We don't talk much, just small observations about the weather and what we will probably order at the cafe. I'm worried that our conversation will turn to sex, but thankfully, I manage to keep it neutral. I am an adult, and I'm very proud of my accomplishments. When we're finally in line at the Food Cafe, I'm thoroughly distracted.

I glance at the menu and my lips turn down. "The prices here are outrageous."

Everly chuckles. "Yeah, they are."

"Soup is ten dollars. Soup. It's basically thick tomato water."

"You going to get a side of free crackers then, old man? Make it worth your while?"

My brow furrows at him, and I purse my lips. "I can afford the thick soupy water, but I don't *want* to afford it."

I glance up at the salads and swing my arm outward. "Fifteen dollars for a small salad? Did they harvest the leaves from some holy place in another country? Jesus."

Everly grins at me and reaches over, clutching the back of my neck. His hands are warm, his fingers strong, and I feel myself melt into him. He should not touch me like this. Who knows what it will do to me below the waist? It's already a treacherous situation.

"Chill, Dr. Sinclair. You're starting to sound like my dad."

"Well, I'm surely old enough to be your father."

He bites his bottom lip and those blue eyes meet mine. "Yeah, but I sure as fuck don't want to suck his dick."

My cheeks flame and my entire body trembles at that. "Keep those thoughts to yourself," I murmur.

He doesn't even look ashamed, and thank god he said those words softly enough that no one heard him.

"Okay, I can do that."

And he does. He keeps those thoughts deep inside of him while we order and while I huff and puff, paying far too much for a minimal amount of food.

He also keeps those thoughts inside when we sit at a booth and he hooks his legs around mine and pretends not to notice that he's doing it.

But then he makes his intentions very well known by the way he licks his spoon. Like he's giving it a blow job and purposefully manages to get mayonnaise on the corner of his mouth, chuckling as he wipes it away.

"You are being inappropriate again," I hiss, and Everly just bats his eyelashes at me.

"I'm just eating. Anything inappropriate is all in your head, Dr. Sinclair."

I scoff at that because the way he's eating his french fries has to be illegal in at least forty states.

"I have lived thirty-five years, I know when someone is trying to entice me with food."

He grins as he licks his way up his straw and sucks it into his mouth.

"I don't know what you mean."

His legs tighten around mine, and I nearly combust on the spot. I can imagine them threaded around me as he pushes inside of me, or surrounding me as he sits on my cock.

"Excuse me. I need to use the restroom," I say, standing up and stalking toward it. I quickly bolt inside the one open stall, trying to steady my breathing. If I keep this up, I'm going to have a stroke. Or a heart attack. Or both.

I glance down at my dick. "You behave."

The man in the stall next to mine grunts as a loud fart exits his ass and echoes around the bathroom. "Tell me about it, dude. My asshole is exploding. Don't get the zucchini fries. You won't get any obedience after that."

My face blanches, and I pull my tie up around my nose and run out to wash my hands. I don't even bother to dry them, just scrub and exit all while holding my breath. As soon as I'm free, I realize that my boner has deflated. Seems explosive diarrhea in a public bathroom will do that to someone. Even my horny dick was deterred.

I glance across the restaurant and see Everly smiling at me, laughing. I pull the tie away from my face and stalk toward him.

"Had quite the experience, didn't you?" Everly asks as I slide into the booth.

"Men are disgusting. I don't know why I'm gay."

He chuckles and runs a hand through his hair, my eyes falling to his biceps. Yes, that's why. He's so fucking hot.

"Well, I do. I love an older man."

I roll my eyes, even though my heart flutters in my chest.

Full Service

"Yes, well, this man is off-limits." I point to myself and then point again. He needs to get the hint.

He scoffs playfully and then links his legs with mine. "I ate some of your salad."

I stare down at the half-empty plate and then glower at him. "Why did you do that?"

"You were picking at it, and I'm a growing boy."

"That's true. Your frontal lobe isn't even fully developed."

A laugh escapes him, and he shakes his head. "Fuck you, Dr. Sinclair. My brain is just fine."

"It's still growing. Some say it doesn't fully develop until men are thirty."

"Ah, so you think I'm too impulsive?"

I do, and for some fucked up reason, I like it. It's dangerous. Maybe my brain is an anomaly and *my* lobe isn't fully formed either.

Would explain a lot actually.

"You are ridiculous, is what you are."

Everly's white teeth flash at me. "You like my kind of ridiculous, though. Admit it."

I clamp my lips closed.

His blue eyes twinkle as he reaches his fork forward and spears some of my salad.

My brows meet as he chews.

"That's my food."

"You aren't eating it."

"I was going to until you got your germs on it."

He swallows and takes another sensual sip of his water. "My tongue was in your mouth earlier and you weren't complaining."

My mouth falls open. "That's because...that's because I hate watermelon. I needed it gone."

His lips crook up. "Gone with the help of my tongue. On yours."

I can feel the tips of my ears turn pink. "We will not mention this again."

I gather my salad closer to me and turn my attention to the green leaves. This is a sad dinner. I'd really have liked a hamburger with fries, but my cholesterol would kill me. Literally.

I stab at them and put them into my mouth, the crunch very unseemly and unsexy.

"Want a bite of my burger?" he asks and then holds it out to me. It's half gone, just a few more bites and he'll have devoured it all.

I shake my head. "No. Germs. I don't want to get sick. You probably have a cold."

"If I do, then you're already infected."

I roll my eyes and keep eating. I don't stop until the bowl is almost licked clean. This salad cost as much as my gas bill. I'm going to eat every chia seed.

"There. All done," I say, and Everly grins at me.

"Good boy."

The way he says it makes my heart thunder in my chest.

"I'm not a *boy*. I'm a grown man. If anyone is a boy, it's you."

He leans forward and rests his head in his hands. "You can say good boy to me anytime. I'm all about it."

I feel my hands start to tremble.

"I will not do any such thing."

There's a five percent chance I won't.

He smirks at me and then leans back. He pops a fry in his mouth and watches me intently.

Even when he chews it's sexy.

"So, what's the plan after this? Any evening classes?"

I shake my head. "I'm just going home. What about you? Work?"

I shouldn't have asked, and yet the words came out anyways. I want to know. I really fucking do.

"Yeah, just a few hours though, and then I can head back to my place. I have a lot of homework to do."

We don't say anything, just watch one another, tension crackling between us.

"You could always stop by and see me. The offer of another dance still stands."

I clear my throat. "We said we'd keep this professional."

"It sure is hard though."

It is. It's ridiculous.

"It's not hard for me."

It's a lie. It's hard for me. I'm hard.

Damn dick hasn't gone down since sitting back down in this booth.

"You sure about that?" he asks, and I glance away from him, straightening my tie.

I'm *not* sure and I know he knows this. So I keep my lips clamped shut.

"Alright, I'll let it go, for now."

"Good. No more talking about this."

I manage a small smile at him, completely false, and Everly waggles his finger in my face. "Got a seed in your teeth."

"For fuck's sake."

I use my tongue to try and get it out, but it's stuck. I need some floss. Or maybe I should just remove my tooth.

That seems viable. A great solution, actually.

"I have something in here," Everly says, rummaging around in his bag, and then pulls out a flosser. I stare at it. It's not even packaged.

"Has this been used?"

"No, fuck off." He laughs. "This was in a package. I carry it around, for work stuff."

"Thanks. I guess having seeds in your teeth doesn't make a good impression."

"They're not usually looking at my teeth, but yeah, I guess not."

I stand up and pull my bag over my crotch, covering my half-hard dick, and make my way to the bathroom. Holding my nose, I quickly get the seed from my teeth.

"Careful. Explosive bombs going off in here," the man calls out from the stall, and I toss the flosser into the trash and jog out of the restroom, nearly bumping into Everly in the process.

"Do not go in there. A biohazard."

"Yeah? Still?"

"Yes. You need a hazmat suit to enter."

Everly chuckles and then nods toward the door. "Let's go get some fresh air then."

We walk out, passing some students mingling on the sidewalk, and I stand a little straighter while moving away from Everly, so no one gets the wrong impression.

The last thing I need is the dean asking me about this. I don't want to be accused of having an inappropriate relationship with my TA.

Even though I kind of am. But then again, professors are allowed to go out to lunch or dinner with students. There's nothing wrong with that.

I've done nothing wrong.

Except continuing to get hard in his presence and letting him stick his tongue in my mouth.

But I just reason it away by saying that it won't happen again. Despite knowing it will.

There's a ninety-nine percent chance it will.

I have no self-preservation and very little strength to resist him, it seems.

Chapter Five

Everly

I definitely know I shouldn't tempt him. I've been playing with fire, toeing the line of professionalism a little too closely. Well, let's be honest here. I've stepped over that damn line a few times. But I didn't hear Dr. Sinclair protesting. He opened his mouth and let me stick my tongue right inside. He didn't even hesitate.

And I don't regret it. He tasted amazing, felt amazing. He's just so hot.

I told you, I have a little bit of an obsession with this guy.

Which is why I'm wearing a gold and black jockstrap under my jeans today.

I bought it just for him.

Technically, I don't have any official plans to meet with Dr. Sinclair today, but I do plan on stopping by his office. A surprise of sorts. Something a TA would *totally* do.

This is just business. With a side of pleasure.

I grin to myself as I make my way toward his building. I don't know if he'll even be there, but it's worth a shot. I really would like to get his opinion on my newest purchase. It's of utmost importance.

Earlier, I sat in my dilapidated apartment, staring at the ceiling which looks as if it will cave in with the next big storm, and contemplated if this thing I'm playing at with Dr. Sinclair is a smart idea. My roommates were gone, and I was eating a stale bagel with questionable cream cheese and really pondering it. I came to the conclusion that I really have nothing to lose at this point. It really can't get much worse than it is.

Growing up, my dad did the best he could as a single parent, and honestly, he's still doing an amazing job, but as a blue-collar worker traveling and living in a small trailer most of the year, there isn't much he can do to help me financially. Hence, the rundown apartment and multiple roommates I currently have.

I shake my head, dislodging the negative thoughts. It's all looking up. I've almost graduated, and pretty soon I'll have a nice place all of my own. Well, maybe not nice, but at least it won't be caving in.

My knuckles land on Dr. Sinclair's closed office door with a small rap. There's no answer, and my heart sinks slightly. I knew it would be a slim chance. He's always busy. Between classes, committee meetings, and grading, I don't expect him to be sitting in his office waiting for me to show up.

But still, my eager heart was ready for him to open it the minute I knocked. Not that he did. He's obviously not here and yet still, I linger.

Leaning against the wall, I pull my phone out, grinning when I see a message from Austin. Yesterday, I finished the book he recommended and he loaned me another one. I'm eager to start it. He tried to give me some spoilers, but I quickly deleted them.

Don't want those, mate. Just want to be surprised.

I respond back to him quickly and then stuff my phone in

Full Service

my pocket, pulling my lips between my teeth as I debate what to do.

Well, if Dr. Sinclair isn't here, I'm not going to just wait around forever like a sad sap. I mean, I totally would, but my time could be spent elsewhere. Like completing the mountains of grading I need to actually focus on.

I push off the wall to head to the library, and just as I do, I hear his voice around the corner. His and another man's.

My mouth falls into a frown before I quickly school my face.

There is absolutely nothing wrong with him speaking to another guy. I'm just unreasonably jealous. This has never happened before, but then again, everything with him is new.

He makes me crazy.

A moment later, the two of them come into view, and I feel my stomach clench. It's the professor from before. The young, handsome one who needed help with his e-mails. I don't even remember his name, but that's irrelevant.

He's cute and more importantly, he's a professor as well.

"Well, Jonah, thank you for walking me to my office," Dr. Sinclair says, his words sputtering off when he sees me. He clears his throat and straightens his tie. "If you have any more questions about that, let me know, and for God's sake, stop locking students out of your classroom."

Jonah flushes slightly and grumbles under his breath. But he nods and turns on his heel, walking away quickly.

As soon as he's gone, Dr. Sinclair's gaze slams into mine.

"Do you need something?" he asks, his voice low and rough.

I do. I need his cock in my ass.

But I don't say that out loud. I just chant it in my mind. Manifestation and all that jazz.

"Just came by to ask a question. A very important one."

Dr. Sinclair's eyebrows rise and he nods, unlocking his office door and gesturing for me to enter.

I do, making sure to purposefully brush past him, our bodies touching for a blissful moment before I finally pull away.

He leaves the door open as I move toward his stuffed bookshelves, and my lips turn down in a scowl. I can't show him my new jockstrap with that damn thing wide open. Jesus. Get a clue, Dr. Sinclair.

"You can close it. It's a very delicate and private matter," I explain, letting my hand fall from the books on the shelves.

Dr. Sinclair's cheeks redden, and he nods. "Of course, student privacy is of utmost importance."

He closes the door with a snick, and I feel my lips twitch in approval. I want to beam, to fucking smile, but I bite it back. He has to take this seriously, and I don't want to give the impression that this is a joke.

He freezes for a moment, his hand on the knob before his finger snakes out and with a flick, locks it.

My heart rate doubles, and I feel my entire body heat.

He's giving me permission. In his own silent way. It makes my dick twitch in my pants. I'm so fucking excited.

Dr. Sinclair clears his throat once more, swipes his hand down his tie, and walks to his chair. His ass lowers into it, and for just a moment, I envision that butt sitting on me.

I want to see it.

I want to strip him bare and lick my way across his entire body and then watch as his dick sinks into me. Balls deep.

"What is it you need that's so delicate and private?" he asks, snapping me out of my lurid thoughts.

"Oh, right." I set my bag down and move toward his desk. "I'd like to ask your opinion about something."

Silas nods and smooths his hand down his chest. That fabulous, broad chest.

"Of course."

I move around the large oak desk and stop near his side. He

swivels his chair so he's facing me, and I rest my hands on my hips.

I can see that he's breathing a little faster, and I want to do this before he changes his mind, unlocks the door, and kicks me out.

"I bought something for work, and I'd like to know what you think."

He doesn't respond, just squeaks slightly. Love it when he makes those noises. Really gets my gears going.

My fingers land on the button of my jeans, and I flick it open. His eyes settle on the movement, and I feel like the hottest performer in town. Shit, he makes me feel like a million bucks.

The zipper is slowly lowered and I spread the fly open, showing him the gold fabric of my jock strap.

His lips part, and he starts to pant.

Mm, yes. I want to see him drool.

"I had to buy this for work, and I don't know if it looks good on me."

It's a ridiculous thing to ask, I know. It looks hot on me, but I'd sure love that reassurance from Dr. Sinclair himself.

My hands tug my jeans down and they pool around my ankles, leaving me standing there, wearing only my t-shirt and my jock strap.

I see the bulge in his slacks as he eyes me.

He's hard. For me.

"What do you think?" I ask, and his eyes flick up to meet mine.

"I can't say with that shirt on."

My mouth splits into a grin as I whip it off.

Now all that's left are my shoes and my pants around my ankles.

He runs a hand across his jaw and lets out a shuddering breath.

"It's nice. Looks good with your skin tone."

I nod, flexing the muscles in my stomach and watching as he lifts a hand, almost as if he's trying to touch me before he curls his fingers into his palm and rests it on the arm of his chair.

"Want to see the back?" I ask, sounding far too innocent. I know exactly what I'm doing.

"Only so I can give you an unbiased opinion."

I snort a small laugh as I turn and flex my glutes, making them round and hard. All those painful squats have been worth it for this moment. I peer over my shoulder at him and see him grind the heel of his palm against his dick.

"What do you think?" I ask. "Do you think people will like it?"

"Yes." It's clipped and strained. "Bend over."

My dick perks up at the sound of his command, and I bend at the waist, letting him take in the view. I wish he'd touch me, stick his face between my cheeks and lick. He's close enough. He totally could, but of course he doesn't.

"Want to see my hole?" I ask, daring him to do something. Anything.

When he doesn't answer right away, I add, "You can touch. See what you think."

He lets out a shaky breath, almost as if warring with himself, and then seconds later, I feel his hands on my ass, warm, strong fingers pulling my cheeks apart so he can see what's hidden inside.

My dick swells even more, achingly hard against the fabric of my jock. His thumbs brush against the straps under each cheek, and I just stand there, completely still, not wanting this to end. I'm worried that if I make a move, he'll realize what he's doing and run.

"Looks very nice," he finally says. It's a rasp more than words, but I'll take the compliment.

I don't respond, just experience this moment. It's going to end soon. He's going to remove his hands from my ass any minute now and the spell will be broken.

But he doesn't. Not as quickly as I expect at least. No, he just holds me, his fingers flexing on my cheeks as I wait with bated breath for what comes next. The air in the office is electric, hot, and thick with tension. I arch my hips back, offering God knows what to him and hoping for acceptance.

He swears under his breath and tightens his grip on me before stuffing his face between my cheeks. I can feel the abrasion from his facial hair hitting my skin, and I shiver just as my mouth opens in a loud gasp.

His face is in my ass.

Holy fuck.

Fuck. Me.

I didn't expect this.

I so fucking didn't.

My hand slams onto the desk beside me to keep myself upright as my legs start to shake. He hasn't even really started rimming me, he's just stuffed his face in there and is breathing me in.

This is by far the hottest thing I've ever done. Or have ever had happen to me.

And it's at the university. In an office. With a professor.

Motherfuck.

A low moan escapes him, soft and desperate, and then his tongue flicks out and swipes over my hole.

I slap my free hand over my mouth to keep myself from groaning loudly. I don't want us to get caught, but *fuuuuuck*, it feels good.

His lips and tongue are teasing my entrance as his fingers grip me roughly. Fuck, I want bruises there tomorrow. I want him to mark me.

His tongue is lapping around my rim, not sliding in but teasing me all the same. I'm frantically trying to keep my moans in, swallowing them down, but it's almost impossible with the way he's taunting me.

I'm so going to get him back for this.

I'm going to figure out a way to make him sit quietly while I take him apart, piece by piece.

My teeth bite down onto my fist as he swirls and flicks his tongue until he finally sighs and plunges into me. My eyelids flutter shut as I arch back into him, wanting him deeper. I want more. A greedy boy.

Who wouldn't be with Dr. Sinclair's tongue up their ass?

It's a slow, methodical fucking. Almost like he's savoring the taste of me. And that in and of itself drives me crazy. I'm gently fucking back against his face as he plunges in and out of me, taking his time, driving me so close to orgasm, and yet it's not enough. I need more. I want his finger up there, his cock.

I'm about to suggest it. I have lube in my bag, but then the phone rings, and Dr. Sinclair swiftly pulls away. It's such a quick, frantic movement that his chair rolls into the wall with a bang.

I clutch at my dick as I turn around and see his chest heaving, his face red and wet.

"Fuck," he whispers, his eyes wide. "Fuck, Everly."

I nod, swallowing as he tries to compose himself. But his arms and legs are shaking and so are mine. We're a trembling mess together. He reaches for the phone and picks it up, clearing his throat and smoothing his tie, his eyes no longer on me.

Quietly, I pull up my pants and tug on my shirt, tucking my still-aching dick under the waistband of my jeans to hide the evidence of what we just did. I want to see if Dr. Sinclair is still hard, but I can't see his cock. He's tucked his legs under the opening of his desk and has hidden himself from me.

Such a goddamn shame.

I want to crawl underneath and suck him into my mouth, listen to him come while on the phone.

But of course, I don't do that. That would be insane.

I straighten my hair and wait for my body to calm down before I grab my bag and start to leave.

Before I do though, I turn around and see Dr. Sinclair watching me, his eyes dark and intent.

Fuck me. He's so hot. I never stood a chance.

I knew it and I went for it anyways.

That night at the club changed *everything*.

I point to the door and he nods, running a hand across the stubble on his face while continuing to speak to someone on the phone. I don't know who it is, nor do I care. I just want them to hang up so we can continue what we started, but I think that's over and done with. The moment of pure insanity was broken as soon as the phone rang, and I honestly don't know if it will ever happen again.

The thought makes me sadder than I care to admit as I pull the door open and stride out.

It's fine. I can hope for more, can try again another time.

If he broke this time, he'll break again.

I'm sure of it.

Chapter Six

Silas

"I'm sorry, you want me to do what?" I ask Lee as we sit outside his small apartment at the home, catching some rays. There's a storm coming in soon and the forecasters have been warning about potential flooding in some counties. But I'm not worried. California has some nice drains that flow rainwater right into the ocean.

"There's a sensual ribbon dance being held here. And my son refuses to join me, and my grandson is far too busy, so I'm asking you to be my wingman."

"Humph, third choice now?"

"Don't be so sour. You're my last hope."

"Jesus," I murmur. "And what the hell even is a sensual ribbon dance?"

"We fling ribbons around while grinding on our walkers."

My eyebrows fly off my face. "I'm not grinding on any walkers. That's indecent."

I don't know what I'm talking about. Walker sex is nothing

compared to sticking my face in Everly's ass and licking his butthole.

Fuck. There's a thirteen percent chance I won't be fired for that.

I need to get my shit together and behave.

I won't do that again.

Yes. Exactly. Never again. Easy peasy.

"You won't use a walker. You still have good knees. You can bend over all on your own. Me, on the other hand, I need some help in that area."

I mean, I can bend over and I do it so well, but I don't tell him that. I just run a hand down my face, contemplating what the hell I'm getting myself into. Because the truth is, I can't say no to him. I'm going to be doing a sensual ribbon dance.

"Fine, I'll do this with you. What kind of commitment is it?"

"Oh well, next week we have a training session, and then you can practice the choreography at home. Or we can practice it here if you want. We can go over our moves together."

"Fuck," I murmur, and when I turn my head to glance at him, I see him grinning wildly. He knows what he's asked me to do. If this is recorded and sent around campus, I'll be the laughingstock. I'll never live it down.

Sensual ribbon dance. Jesus fucking Christ.

"We're going to have a blast, Silas. Just you wait."

"If I see you humping your walker, I will walk off stage and never return."

He chuckles and leans his head back. "I do what I want, young man. Nothing you can do to stop me. Plus, I have some ladies to impress in the audience."

"Oh, dear God. Please dig out my eardrums," I murmur.

"It could be a mating dance," he continues, and I plug my ears, trying to keep his words out. If he tells me he's been having sex, I will get up and leave. I will not stay for that. I don't want to think about old, shriveled dicks and ball sacs.

"Don't worry. I won't tell you how rampant the sex life is here. That's between me and the walls."

"Good God, Lee. At least tell me that you're using protection."

"Meh, I have a few good years left. I'm not worried."

My eyes bug out of my head. "Lee. That is a terrible mindset."

"My mind won't be here much longer anyways."

I reach out and shove him lightly. Don't want to actually hurt him. He grabs my hand, squeezing it between his arthritic fingers.

"I'm just kidding, Silas. Don't worry. I know you don't have anyone, and I'm going to hang in there as long as I can. I promise."

My eyes sting, and I swallow the lump in my throat. He's right. I have been on my own for so very long. I rarely talk to the family I have left.

I'm closer with Lee than any of them.

What does that say about me?

We stare out into the distance and watch the clouds roll in and when the first raindrop hits, we move back inside. It's a steady downpour, so instead of eating outside, we grab lunch in the main hall.

This is a nice facility. They have all sorts of things for older adults, like a hair and nail salon and a pretty damn good restaurant all within walking distance. They even have a nice coffee bar, but the coffee isn't nearly as good as the coffee on Franklin U's campus.

Well, either that or I just really like it when Everly brings me a sweet coffee to sip on.

Or his ass to eat.

My dick twitches in my pants and I poke at it, trying to get it to behave. I don't need Lee thinking that I'm turned on by someone here. He'd never let me live it down.

And I really need to stop thinking about my TA like that.

I lost my mind the other day, but it won't happen again.

We get settled at a small table that overlooks the gardens and the bocce ball court and place our orders with one of the staff. I, of course, get my salad while Lee gets a hamburger and fries. And as he orders, I bite back my chiding.

He's not a child, but fuck, he acts like one sometimes.

"It took a lot of restraint for you to keep those comments to yourself, I can tell," Lee says and grins at me. "Your face is red."

I roll my eyes and let out a long breath. "I'm growing as a person."

Lee snorts and takes a sip of his coffee. Don't get me started on how little water he drinks, for fuck's sake. He's probably as dry as the desert in those old veins of his.

"So, tell me about your love life. Gone down on any hot men lately?"

"Jesus, Lee."

"My grandson told me about a fun online site, and I've been reading up on all the dirty slang. Apparently snowballing isn't what I thought it was."

I shake my head as a laugh explodes out of me. "Your grandson is a menace."

"That he is," he says and then leans forward. "I can give you his number, if you want."

"No thank you," I say, my mind flashing to Everly. I have enough to handle with him. I can't imagine adding in another rowdy young guy. I would probably die from the stress of it.

Lee huffs and leans back in his chair, almost pouting. "Fine, he's too young for you anyways. How about my son's number then?"

Full Service

"I didn't think he was gay?"

"He's not. Well, not that I know of, but he is lonely and you're a good-looking guy. I bet you two would hit it off."

"Lee," I say with a huff of laughter. "That's not how it works."

"It should work that way, but fine. I guess I'll have to settle with you not being part of my family by law. Just in my heart."

His statement makes my own heart thunder in my chest. He's always doing this, as if he knows how badly I need some kind of parental connection. I've only known him a few months, but I feel like I've known him for years. We have a lot in common, and from the small amount of time I've spent with him, I've learned so much about myself.

I'm a better man because of him.

The food is set down before us, and I stare glumly at the bowl of leaves.

"Would you like a fry?" Lee asks, and I begrudgingly take it from him and pop it into my mouth.

"These are extra salty. They must be terrible for your kidneys," I grumble.

"Sperm has salt in it as well, and yet you don't hear me telling you to stop sucking dick."

The fry lodges in my throat and I choke, my body tensing up as my esophagus contracts in an attempt to get it down the pipe. I gulp down some water and thankfully don't die on the spot, my watering eyes catching Lee grinning like the loon he is.

"Are you trying to kill me?"

"Of course not, just telling it like it is."

"For fuck's sake. Keep those little facts to yourself," I say as I swipe at my wet eyes. "And if you must know, it's not salt in ejaculate. It's sodium. Not the same thing."

Lee waggles his eyebrows at me, and I sigh, realizing that he gives zero shits. His comment was just to rile me up, and his mission has been accomplished.

We eat the rest of our food, chattering about nothing important, just the gossip happening in his life and here in the home. I tell him briefly about my sister and niece and then a little more about my job at the university.

Suddenly, a man with ribbons dangling off his bare arms and legs appears and confidently struts toward us.

I sink down into my seat and hold my breath.

Jesus. It's sensual-ribbon-man. If I don't move, maybe he won't be able to see me.

"Hello there, Mr. O'Conner," the man says, waving his arm around his head, the ribbons fluttering around him. "Did you find a partner for the dance?"

"Sure did," Lee says as he points to me. "This distinguished man right here."

"Ah." The man's dark eyes rove over me, and I feel myself blushing. He's handsome in his own way, probably around my age and has nice skin, but he's just a little bit too...much for someone like me.

I'd much prefer the subtle, ruggedly handsome looks of Everly. And his ass. And chest and face. Really all parts of Everly leave my dick hard and aching.

Not that I'll ever see those parts of him again.

I'm drawing the line. A long and thick one.

No more crossing the goddamn line.

"I'm LoveJoy," the man says, holding his ribboned fingers out toward me.

My eyes widen slightly at his name, but I bite my tongue once more. What kind of name is that? Jesus fucking Christ on a cracker.

"Hello, I'm Silas."

I wrap my hand around his and he pumps it a little too long before he finally lets go of me.

Lee finds it necessary to pipe up. "It's actually Dr. Silas Sinclair. He's a professor."

LoveJoy's eyes widen with interest. "Oh, I love a smart man."

"Hm," is all I can say. I don't want to encourage him and his obvious interest in me. He may tie me down with ribbons and subject me to a creepy dance. One that I definitely don't want.

The only one who should be dancing for me is Everly.

"So nice to meet you, *Doctor*."

He purrs the last word and then flutters his arms all around, the ribbons whipping up a frenzy as he moves. I glower at Lee, who is grinning happily at me. He's loving every second of this, that fucker.

"I can't wait to help you both come up with a routine. It will be such fun."

"Oh, I can't wait either," Lee says with a chuckle and then runs a hand over his mouth—trying to conceal his laughter, I'm sure.

LoveJoy continues to flutter around us, and I swear, it's like he's never going to stop, but finally, he gets called away and pouts as he turns to leave. But not before pulling a ribbon off and tying it around my wrist.

"To remember me by," he says softly, and I stare at the blue, shimmering ribbon with a frown.

I don't want to remember him or his ribbons. I want to forget this ever happened.

"I think that went well," Lee says, and I glower at him, sending him death rays with my eyeballs.

"I'm going to smother you in your sleep, old man."

"You'd never. You secretly want to be a part of this ribbon dance and flirt some more with LoveJoy."

"I do not," I huff and then let out a chuckle. Why is this my life? I swear to God. This would only happen to me.

When it's finally time to leave, it's still pouring out. Jogging to my car, I nearly slip on the ground, but catch myself in a very ungraceful waggling of limbs before sliding into my car, half-soaked. I don't know when this storm is supposed to pass, but I'm annoyed already. I didn't settle here in Southern California for it to rain. I want sun. All year long.

I have expectations, damnit.

I drive back to my place and park the car in the small garage, thankful that I decided to drive today and not walk. If I'd done that, I'd have been soaked to the bone.

As soon as I enter my living room, I pull off my tie, reach into my pocket, and toss the ribbon onto the end table. I should throw it away but worry this damnable thing actually means something to creepy LoveJoy.

I stare at the fish tank and see Vertebrata staring at me. "Hello, fish."

She blinks at me and then swims away, showing me her tail as she hides under her coral. I really, really need to find her a friend. Someone like LoveJoy, who will flutter around her space and force her to engage in sensual fish swimming.

I snort as I unbutton my shirt and move to the kitchen, pouring myself a glass of wine. My mind wanders to Everly, and I wonder what he's doing right now. Is he in class? Studying? Or is he at the club dancing?

I most certainly shouldn't go there in this weather to check. I drew the line already. With permanent marker. I won't be crossing it again.

I pull my shirt off all the way and toss it onto the couch, running a hand down my warm skin and straight down into my pants.

I should definitely not get off to thoughts of him again, but I do. I end up on my bed, my leg pulled up to my chest, a vibrating dildo up my ass as I fuck my hand.

And of course, Everly is the one on my mind, his beautiful ass on display, the smell of him, the taste. I explode across my bare chest with his name on my lips and then lie there in my own blissful shame until I finally fall asleep.

I didn't cross a line doing that.

I most definitely didn't.

But even so, I won't be doing it again.

* * *

The rain hasn't stopped. It's been carrying on like a drama queen, not even letting up for a minute. Just a constant, steady downpour overnight and into the next day. Some professors have canceled classes, but I refuse. A little rain never hurt anyone.

Or so I think.

Until I stride into the library and see Everly at a desk in the corner with a very handsome athletic man in a basketball jersey and shorts. And the man is wet, nearly dripping, looking like sex incarnate. Like he just stepped out of a shower and forgot his towel.

My ass twinges and flexes, remembering that dildo up my ass last night, pretending it was Everly's cock. How pathetic. I'm thirty-five, old and tired. And here Everly is, not thinking about me at all. No, he's leaning forward and pressing far too close to another man his own age. I notice Everly's shirt is wet, his hair too, like he stood in the rain a little too long.

My cock twitches, obviously not getting the hint that Everly is preoccupied with a younger and much hotter man than me.

I force my gaze away and make my way down another aisle, only occasionally peering through the books at him, watching as he laughs softly at something the other man says and lays his hand on his forearm.

Something ugly and mean surges up inside of me.

I don't own him, don't have any right to feel this way, and yet I do.

Something in my brain yells that he's mine.

Mine.

I force my gaze away and continue walking aimlessly down the aisle, having completely forgotten why I was here in the first place. I rack my brain, trying to remember what in the hell I'm doing in the library.

In a moment of clarity, I remember that I was going to request a book from another university and with a somewhat sound mind, I make my way back up to the front desk. But not before glancing over my shoulder and watching as the guy presses his forehead to Everly's shoulder and Everly gently pats his head.

This is too much PDA for the library. This is a scholarly environment.

I should sound an alarm.

But before I can, Everly glances up at me and I quickly turn away, forcing myself to not turn back around and glower. I refuse. I will not show him how annoyed I am that he's touching someone else.

I'm an adult.

This is not how someone my age behaves.

So with straight shoulders, I place my order with the front desk and then with purposeful steps make my way through the rain and back to my office, where I sit in my chair and pout.

I should be working, should be answering emails, or even grading, but instead, I just stare at the door and frown.

Stupid Everly and his stupid ass.

Of course that jock is attracted to him. Everly is hot, incinerating. Any and all straightness that guy may have felt would have been burned right off. And of course Everly is interested in a muscled athlete. That's probably his type. Not boring old me who eats salads and wears ugly ties to work.

My hand runs down my face, and I stare at the clock. I have class in an hour and I need to prep, but I have zero motivation.

I just want to sit here and sulk like the child I've become.

This is good though, I try to reason with myself. This is the line I drew very carefully. He's not crossing it anymore, especially since he's into someone else now.

This is a good thing.

The best thing, really.

I turn on my computer and pull up my email, seeing an urgent one from the school, reminding me that I have a sexual harassment training module that I need to complete.

Well, if that isn't a cold, harsh reminder. What I've done with Everly is *wrong*. I need to remember not to do it again, no matter how tempting he is.

I need to remember that I cannot sexually harass my TA by sticking my tongue up his hole.

Suddenly, there's a knock on the door. I sit up a little straighter in my seat and place my hands on my keyboard, wanting to look like I'm actually working and not ruminating over a student.

And harassing him in my brain.

"Come in," I say gruffly, and a moment later, a very wet Everly strides into my office.

My hands slide off the keyboard and my mouth falls open. Fuck. His t-shirt is practically see-through. I can see his hard nipples and the outline of his belly button. This is terrible. Absolutely wretched. That line I drew is looking a little squiggly at the moment.

With very large gaps in-between.

Ones I could easily walk through.

"Where in God's name is your sweater?" I hiss, and Everly glances down at himself and shrugs.

"I forgot it at home."

I snap my mouth shut and grind my teeth. "It's torrential out there!"

"Yeah, I didn't realize it was storming until after I left my place. Didn't have time to run back."

"There's been warnings all over the news for days."

"Who listens to the news, old man?"

I scoff and motion to the door. "Close it."

Everly reaches behind him and pushes it shut. He stands there, positively dripping as I stand and rummage through a box behind my desk.

A moment later, I hand over a t-shirt and a sweater from the biology club I was an advisor for that I never could get rid of. They've just been sitting here for years, collecting dust.

"Change into this before you catch cold."

"Are these yours?" he asks, and I swallow. I would like to see him in some of my clothes, not that I'll ever allow that.

No.

Lines.

I have *lines*.

"No. They're just extras from the club that I never threw away."

"Cool. Vintage." Everly takes them from my hands, and I feel the cold tips of his fingers. He must be freezing.

I should turn around and not watch him strip that shirt off. But I don't. I just wait for him to pull it off, like the pervert I've become, staring at his puckered, pink nipples before they're sadly covered with the dry fabric. Within seconds, he has the sweater on, looking far too good in something cheesy that I purchased wholesale.

Full Service

I bet he could make a napkin look brilliant.

I'd very much like to see that.

"Thanks," he says and then runs a hand through his wet hair.

I sigh and rummage around in the box once more, pulling out another shirt and bringing it up to his head and scrubbing at it. It's not a towel, but it'll do.

"Do you honestly not have an umbrella?" I ask, standing far too close to him. He smells like rain and wind and fucking sex.

He swallows, and his eyes slide down to my lips, his body trembling slightly. "No. Who owns an umbrella in Southern California?"

"Adults," I reply and step a little closer to him, our bodies brushing. Everly lets out a stuttered breath, smelling like mint. Like a nice piece of candy.

I want to gobble him up.

"You should really own one."

"Do you have one for me lying around in here?"

I let my hands fall to his shoulders, and he leans toward me.

"No. But you need one. You're going to catch a cold walking around like this," I say, my voice nearly a whisper.

"If I get sick, will you take care of me, Dr. Sinclair?"

The way he says my name, a whisper against my lips makes my entire body flame. My hands slide down his bulky arms, feeling the way those muscles move beneath my fingertips before quickly pulling away.

If I keep touching him, there's a good chance that I'll end up bent over my desk and begging. And I can't do that.

"If you were on death's door, I would," I reply and then take a step back. "But you're an adult, you can take care of yourself."

"I get very needy when I'm sick. I never had a mom growing up."

My eyes flash to his, and I see his bottom lip jut out. "What do you mean?"

He shrugs. "She left when I was a baby. It's just been me and my dad. And he was always working. When I was sick, I was left to fend for myself."

"I didn't realize," I say, and Everly smiles at me.

"It's fine. How could you? We're practically strangers." He lowers his voice. "Even though you did have your tongue in my ass."

My cheeks flame, and I feel my cock perk up. I did. My tongue was all up in him.

"That is very inappropriate."

"So is rimming your TA in your office," he teases, and my face falls.

"You're right," I say, taking a step back and walking on shaky legs to my chair. I sit down and run a hand down my tie. "That was inappropriate. Everything about this is. And it won't be happening again. I temporarily lost sight, and my mind, but it won't happen again."

"Dr. Sinclair—" Everly begins, but I stop him with a slash of my hand. I'm glad he said that. I'm remembering that I need to get my shit together. This very well could get me fired, and I can't risk it all for a goddamn boy.

"I could lose my job, Everly," I hiss and then shake my head. "You should go."

His shoulders slump slightly. "Come on. It was a joke. You can violate me anytime. Seriously."

My cheeks burn, and I sit stiffly in my chair.

"Won't happen again. Goodbye, Mr. Winslow."

He sighs, and in my periphery I see him run a hand through his damp hair again.

"Right, okay. I get it. I got it. See you soon."

He turns and disappears from my office, probably off to do

God-knows-what with God-knows-who. That's fine. It's more appropriate anyways. Anyone he fucks around with will at least be his age. And that's good for him.

And very good for me.

Because I should definitely not be lusting after him, and I most assuredly should not be putting my face anywhere near his ass again. If he reports me, I'll deserve any discipline that comes my way.

That's right. I need to remember I could get in trouble for this. For acting like a sex-starved man with someone who is clearly a student. The power imbalance is insane. Not only that, but he's my TA, for fuck's sake.

This is for the best. He can have his jock, and I'll make sure this remains professional between us from now on.

No more sitting outside his place of work.

And most definitely no more jacking off to thoughts of him.

Chapter Seven

Everly

Dr. Sinclair put his foot down. And it wasn't on my dick like I would have preferred. A nice foot caress on my cock to rub one out would have been nice. I could see him doing that, reaching his socked toes out and rubbing them up and down my hard length.

Fuck. Me. I'd be so here for that.

Yeah, but no, there was no cock touching. Instead, he shut this thing between us down. He hasn't even shown up to the club in days. Hasn't waved to the bouncer as he strolled casually by. Hasn't even sat in the parking lot and waited for me. Where the hell did my Sneaky Stalker Sinclair go? I want him back.

And honestly, how could he lick my ass and then tell me that it won't happen again? He can't give me a taste of him and then pull away. That's not fair. The whole thing really gets my competitive juices flowing.

I want him.

I want his tongue on me again.

His hands. His eyes.

I want them to slide across me while I stand there, aching and needy. I want it all.

And he told me motherfucking *no*.

I lean against the wall, my phone sitting uselessly in my hand. I have tutoring to get to with Garrett, but I don't want to go. I'd rather stand outside the biology building and try to catch sight of Dr. Sinclair. Not that he's here. He's been avoiding me. Probably knows I'm lurking around outside and is hiding in his office.

Fuck.

I run a hand through my hair and then stride toward the library where I plan to meet Garrett for our session. I met him when I first transferred here, and we hit it off. We had a short fling before we realized we weren't compatible, but we decided to remain friends. When he reached out to me for private tutoring last week, I couldn't turn him down. He's not part of the biology classes I normally TA for, but I'm helping him with his English Lit class. It's not his forte and happens to be something I'm not half bad at. I do love reading.

Love all that delicious smut Austin keeps recommending to me.

My eyes turn back to the biology building, and I run a hand across my jaw. I just want to stand here and wait for Dr. Sinclair to come out and then crowd him until he caves. Again.

But I can't do that. I need to get to Garrett, the guy Dr. Sinclair glowered at when he saw us together. He looked pretty pissed actually.

My heart skips a beat in my chest.

You know what? Come to think of it, in that moment, he seemed a little jealous.

I stand up straighter, my mind spinning. Oh fuck. Was he jealous?

What if he was?

Maybe I could make him even more so. Show him what he's missing.

Me. That's what he's missing.

I move toward my meeting spot with a purpose I haven't felt before. I know what I have to do. I know what I have to ask of my friend.

As soon as I see Garrett, his mouth splits into a wide smile, and I slide into the seat next to his, dropping my bag on the floor.

"Hey, how are you?" I ask and bump his meaty fist.

"Good. You're late."

I roll my eyes. "Had a bit of stalking to do."

He bobs his head, his brown hair flopping into his eyes. He leans back and folds his large arms across his barrel chest. "Right on. Who are you stalking?"

"Someone kind of forbidden," I say, and Garrett sits up a little straighter.

"Oh yeah? Who? I love forbidden shit. Especially if it's illegal."

"Ha. None of your business."

He waggles his eyebrows at me. "I'd love for it to be my business."

I glance around and then lean forward. "I mean, you *could* help me."

Garrett bites his lip in excitement, his dark brown eyes twinkling. His hands rub together and he wiggles in his seat.

"Are we making someone jealous? Who?"

"Yeah. We're gonna make my stalker jealous. If you're okay with that."

"I'm so down. So, are we stalking your stalker too? Love this shit. And I *am* pretty hot. I can make all the gays green with jealousy. Bi's too. I mean, I am one, so there's that."

"Jesus," I say with a laugh. "No, I'm not stalking my stalker, but yeah, please help me out. Work some of that Garrett magic on him."

"I *so* can. And I won't get to know who this special dude is, right?"

"Nope. It's my secret."

He leans in and nuzzles my neck. "I gotchu. I'll make him wild with rage, even if I have no clue who it is. I'll be on my best flirty behavior. I'll even start now."

He pecks a kiss to my cheek before sitting back and cracking his knuckles. "Alright. Now help me with my shit. You owe me."

If this plan works, I sure as fuck do.

Chapter Eight

Silas

Not jacking off to thoughts of Everly has been painfully hard, but I've managed to keep my dick under control. Staying away from him is tougher than it should be though. He seems to be almost flaunting that unnamed athletic guy in front of me. The hot one he was talking to in the library the other day. The one that kept touching him and smiling at him and being far too flirty. I should know his name because he's probably one of my students, but let's be real.

I don't know any of my students' names. Just a select few who make an impression. Although, hot jock guy has been making a terrible impression. I look for him in my classes, my eyes scanning the crowds like a hawk, but I don't see him. He must be in the large introduction course and must sit way in the back. Probably sleeps through my lectures, which is why he needs help from Everly.

He doesn't deserve him.

And neither do you.

And yet despite reminding myself of this, the next few days, I see the two of them *everywhere*.

And when I say everywhere, I mean it. Literally not an hour goes by where they're not somewhere in my peripheral.

It's disgusting. They should really keep their handsy public displays of affection to themselves. It's indecent.

Not that they're doing anything particularly bad, but the way that jock looks at Everly makes me want to cut out my eyeballs. I really should, so I don't have to be tempted by Everly anymore.

Or jealous.

Because that's what I am. I'm fucking jealous. And it's ridiculous.

I've done so well the past week, behaving like the adult I should be. And Everly's just been lurking around with Hottie McHotButt, with those big muscles, full head of hair and youthful face. Jock-guy doesn't look tired at all. He looks energetic and happy, like he could have a sex marathon without throwing his back out and his balls falling off.

I force my frowning lips to move into a neutral grimace as I stand before my class.

There. That's better.

I can be happy. I am the *happiest*.

Everly is currently hugging the jock at the door to the classroom and my hands tighten on the podium top, the wood creaking under my grip.

They're whispering to one another, their faces far too close. The torrential rain finally let up a few days ago, but it's cold out, and a cool gust of wind floats through the open door. I feel it all the way down to where I'm standing. As a shiver moves through me, I watch as a student squeezes past them, trying to get into the room.

Full Service

Good God. They're blocking the entrance. This is a fire hazard.

Not to mention an environmental one. All the heat in the room is escaping. We're contributing to global warming. The polar ice caps are currently melting at a faster rate.

"Mr. Winslow," I blurt, my voice booming loudly. Students in the front row startle, a pencil flying up into the air, as Everly turns his gaze toward me. Almost as if he didn't notice I was here. Well, of course he didn't notice. Not when he has *that* draped all over him. "Please move your canoodling away from the door."

"Canoodling," a student giggles, and I glower at her. She shrivels back into her seat like the raisin she is.

"Yes, canoodling," I emphasize and then point my gaze back to Everly, who seems unbothered by my little outburst. He almost looks like he's fighting off a grin. That fucker.

But at least he does what I ask. The door closes behind him, and the jock disappears outside. I swear, I don't know which class of mine that kid is in.

My eyes watch as Everly saunters down the aisle to the small desk at the front of the room. He looks delicious in his worn jeans and fitted sweater. I do not stare too long, but I do occasionally glance his way. Sue me. He's irresistible.

But he doesn't glance over at me. He took my stern words the other day to heart. We're keeping this professional from now on. No more lusting after my TA. No more ass-licking.

So, this is good. I do not want him looking at me.

Not at all.

I don't need the temptation. Especially since I've been doing so well.

And yet, through the entire lecture, I find my eyes straying toward him, and the grimace on my face turns into a frown. Especially when class ends. After answering students' questions, he strides out of the room without a backward glance. He doesn't even look at me when he leaves.

This is fine. This is perfectly reasonable.

I told him that everything needed to stop and it has. That line is firmly in place. Just like it should be.

I won't be getting fired anytime soon, which is a great thing. The best thing really.

But at the same time, I won't be seeing Everly's ass either. Which is absolutely wonderful. His ass does terrible things to my brain. Makes me lose all reason and do inappropriate things.

Maybe jock-man is doing inappropriate things to Everly's ass now. Maybe Everly has forgotten all about me.

Which is great. I don't mind that *at all*.

I grab my satchel and stomp from the room, pulling my coat closed across my chest as the cold air pelts me. The forecast has more rain on the horizon. After the last storm, I'm very much *not* looking forward to the next one. Students use the rain as a reason to not attend class, and I hate teaching to empty seats.

My feet suddenly stumble to a stop when I see Everly and the jock in the distance, his hands lifting a scarf off his own neck and wrapping it around Everly's neck.

That is definitely something a boyfriend would do.

They have to be together.

Everly grins at the jock and then pulls him in for a hug before pulling away and walking in the opposite direction. The jock watches him, his hands in his pockets, his feet rocking him back and forth, his lips pulled between his teeth.

He's probably eyeing Everly's behind. I don't blame him. It's very...round. The perfect peach and just as sweet.

I move toward him, and as I stride past, I bump against him, making him stumble slightly to the side.

It was an accident. I'd never purposefully do that to a student.

"Oh, shit, watch where you're going," the guy says and then clears his throat. "I mean, sorry, Dr. Sinclair."

I don't know why he's apologizing. I'm the one who ran into him in a jealous rage.

No, not a jealous rage. Just an accident.

Totally an accident.

"It's fine," I say and then before I can stop myself, I ask, "So, you and my TA, huh?"

The jock grins, not looking shy at all.

"Oh yeah. He's wild."

My eyebrows meet in frustration. What does he mean? I need a definite answer so I can put this to rest. Not that my jealousy will subside. Seems to be raging at the moment. And will forever and ever.

"Hm, well, congrats," I murmur as I pull my satchel further over my shoulder and turn to walk away. I can feel the kid's eyes on me, probably wondering what my deal is. But it doesn't matter. I need to find someone my own age.

Lee's voice comes into my mind. Apparently LoveJoy has been asking about me. He wants my phone number. Perhaps I should give sensual-ribbon-man a chance. Maybe he isn't all that terrible in real life. Maybe we'll have a real connection.

God, I need to get a life if I'm actually considering a date with LoveJoy. Even his name sounds like a candy.

But later that day, in a moment of pure desperation, I call Lee and ask for LoveJoy's number. What could it hurt? Maybe he gives great head. Who knows? Maybe he's my soulmate. Because it's most definitely not Everly.

It can't be.

Lee's happily wheezing when I hang up on him. Apparently, he found me asking for LoveJoy's number hysterical. Well, laugh it up, old man. Not everyone can be as lucky as him to have found the love of his life early on.

I'm practically on my way out. I need to get shit moving if I want a chance of finding someone.

I will. One day.

And it most certainly won't be Everly Winslow.

* * *

"Hello, Dr. Sinclair," Everly says the next day as he comes into my office. It's the first time he's been in here since I told him that we need to keep things professional, that whatever this is between us is essentially over. And this is the first time he's actually spoken to me.

Although, he's not making eye contact.

Which bothers me more than it should.

Why the hell isn't he looking at me? Is there something suddenly wrong with my face? I mean, I *have* been tired and *very* sexually frustrated, but I can't look that bad. LoveJoy is into me. Or at least that's what Lee told me between cackles.

And he gave me his ribbon. Must mean something.

Could be a marriage proposal.

Still haven't called him though. I haven't had the stomach for it.

"Hello, Mr. Winslow," I say and smooth my hand down my tie.

Everly moves to the small desk in the corner of my office and sets his bag down, pulling his phone out and staring at the screen.

He didn't even bring me coffee. Not that he should. It's terrible for my blood sugar. But still, it's very thoughtless on his part.

"How are you?" I ask, and he shrugs, his thumb swiping across the screen. Probably on some dating app. Probably has a long line of people he's sleeping with now.

My dick perks up at the thought of Everly in bed, completely naked and bouncing on my dick.

Good God. I shouldn't have gone into Everly-celibacy cold turkey. Not jacking off at all was a mistake. I need some relief, especially when he smells so damn good. Is that cologne or just some kind of soap he uses? His deodorant?

Whatever it is, it's making me horny.

"I don't read body language," I grumble. "Words are preferable."

His eyes peek up at me and then slash back to his screen. "I'm fine. Been busy with…Garrett. Doing some beach cleanups. You know, saving planet Earth."

My jaw pops from clenching tightly. Of course he's been busy with jock-man. Of course not only is he athletic, but he's apparently Captain Planet as well. That fucker.

"Is Garrett that jock who was all over you the other day?" I ask, even though I mean *every day*. That man is all up in Everly's business.

"Yeah."

Everly shifts in his seat and opens his mouth to say something else but a line of students starts to filter into my office, and we get to work. It's endless until my office hours are over, and I only have time to glance over at Everly every five minutes. But every time I do, he doesn't even look my way. I bet he's forgotten I exist. I would forget I exist too if I had a beefy Garrett all up on me.

Speaking of the big man, he shows up at the end of office hours and strides over to Everly in my office and nuzzles up against him, making my entire body stiffen in anger. Honestly, they really should get a room.

If they start kissing in front of me, I will flip the table over.

But before they can start, Everly pulls away and then grabs his bag.

"You ready to go, babe?" Garrett says, and I find myself frowning when his hand goes down and grabs Everly's ass. I'm pretty sure my face is going to stick like this if I keep this up.

"Can you keep your hands to yourself?" I grind out when he doesn't let go of Everly's butt.

Garrett chuckles and removes his fingers from Everly. "Yeah, sorry about that. It's just a hot ass."

It is.

Everly laughs loudly and shoves at Garrett. "Stop it."

"Come on, babe. I want to touch it," Garrett whines, and my nostrils flare.

"Take that outside," I grumble, and Everly glances at me and...was that a wink he just threw my way? I'm going to fire him.

How inconsiderate. Is he mocking me? Showing me what I'm missing? Because I already know what I'm missing.

Him.

I'm missing him.

The two of them disappear from sight, and I sink down in my chair, running a hand over my face. I need to get a grip.

Suddenly, in this moment, a date with LoveJoy sounds like a great plan. He will help me forget all about Everly.

Chapter Nine

Silas

"Are you ready for our first practice," Lee says, sitting on his walker and rubbing his hands together. I forgot that I had to be here today. If I'd remembered this practice, I wouldn't have asked Lee for LoveJoy's number. It would have saved me from the constant ribbing he's been giving me about it ever since.

"I'm not. I still don't know what sensual ribbon dancing is."

"Neither do I. I think LoveJoy made it up, but I'm ready for it all."

"Jesus," I murmur as LoveJoy makes his way into the room. A dozen or so residents start chattering excitedly when they see him, and my eyebrows meet when I take in what he's wearing. Is that a ribbon shirt? I don't fucking know. All I know is that I can see his nipples and bellybutton.

"Good morning, young ladies and gents!" he says, waving his ribboned arms around. "Who's ready to learn some nasty, filthy moves?"

Everyone hoots in excitement, and I sink further into my

chair. I most definitely do not want to see these people doing anything nasty. That will haunt my nightmares for ages to come. I glance to my right and see a young woman about my age. Our eyes meet and she smiles sadly at me.

"This is our life now," she says softly, and I nod.

"Damnit."

She chuckles and then turns her head back to face LoveJoy, who is instructing everyone to stand up. I do so reluctantly and watch as Lee grins at me maniacally. He knows exactly what sensual ribbon dancing is and knows exactly what he's gotten me into. He's living for this.

LoveJoy hands out several ribbons for us to wave around and then instructs us on some very basic dance moves. My admiration for him grows slightly in these moments. He's chosen moves these old folks can do easily and doesn't expect too much. It's very sweet, actually.

But when his eyes settle on me and he hops in my direction, I slink back. I don't want any of his sweetness directed at me.

Asking for his number was a huge mistake. Not jerking off for a few days has made me a mad man.

"Hello, Dr. Sinclair. So glad you're here." He taps my hips. "You're more flexible than you'd think," he says very flirtatiously. "You can bend over and shake that ass."

My cheeks flame, and Lee cackles next to me.

I'm going to murder him. I'll so go to jail for this.

"I'm not shaking my ass," I grind out. "Absolutely not."

"But you should. Wave your ribbon like this when you do it," he says and gives me a very long demonstration. Lee is clapping loudly next to me and everyone else joins in when they see him bouncing his ass cheeks. It's very impressive actually. I don't know how he does it. They move independently of each other.

Full Service

When LoveJoy finally stands up, he takes a bow and then announces loudly that it's my turn to give it a shot.

I refuse.

But when everyone starts chanting my name, I'm forced to do it. My hands are waving the ribbons around as I bend over and shake my ass. Just once. The cheers I hear make me feel like I've just won the Super Bowl.

These fuckers.

I hate my life.

Doesn't help that my face has completely melted off by the end of practice and I can't make eye contact with anyone. Although the young woman who looked just as perturbed by this as me, pats me on the shoulder and then makes the sign of the cross near my face.

"We will survive this," she tells me, and I sigh.

I want to go home, crawl into my refrigerator, and never come out.

But I can't go home yet. I have another class to teach. Another class that Everly will be in. Fuck. Me. I'll have to stand up there in front of all those students and give my lecture with his hot ass right in my sight.

"So, Saturday?" LoveJoy says suddenly, breaking me out of my very inappropriate thoughts.

"Huh?" I ask, feeling his hand on my arm. He squeezes it gently before I pull away, needing some space. His touch doesn't feel right.

He's not *him*.

"Saturday. For our date. Lee told me how excited you are."

He grins, and for a moment, looks kind of cute with his kind eyes and glossy lips before a ribbon flutters past my face. Ah yes. Ribbons.

Ribbon-man.

"Yes," is all I can say, and LoveJoy bites his lip.

"Great," he says as he pulls his phone out. "Phone number?"

I don't want to give it to him, but what's my other option? Everly? No.

Not him.

I rattle off my digits, and LoveJoy grins widely. My own phone pings a second later, and I glance down and see that he's messaged me.

"I'll pick the place?" he asks, and I nod.

"Sure."

He claps his hands and then presses a kiss to my cheek. He smells like cotton candy.

"See you soon, Dr. Sinclair." He practically purrs my name, and I feel myself wanting to melt into a puddle. This is so not going to go well.

I am in deep shit.

* * *

What makes it even worse is that Everly looks so damn hot tonight. I don't know what he's done differently, but I'm having a very hard time keeping my dick in my pants. It keeps wanting to jump out and into my hand.

I really need to get off. Tonight. No more celibacy. It's not working.

This is an emergency.

Pheromones are a real thing. Maybe he's exuding more than normal tonight.

Maybe he's potent to me.

I definitely don't get this way around LoveJoy. I shudder and then peer over at Everly, who is typing on his laptop at his seat in the classroom. Those deft fingers move quickly, and I imagine them trailing up my chest and into my mouth. I'd suck on them as his other hand cups my balls.

Full Service

My voice squeaks and laughter flutters around me. I feel my face heat, but clear my throat and continue on. I should win the Nobel Peace Prize for teaching this subject matter with a massive erection.

If I can do this, world peace is definitely in the cards.

When class is finally over, Everly moves toward me, and I stay exactly where I am. If I step away from the podium, people will see the massive dick outline in my slacks.

"I've graded all the quizzes," he says, and my eyes nearly roll back into my head at the smell of him. This is insanity. There's no reason for me to behave this way. It has to be biological.

"Is there anything else you want from me?"

His eyes flick up to meet mine and for the first time in a long time he's looking directly at me. My heart flutters terribly in my chest and my cock positively leaks.

I want to push him to the ground, pull my dick out, and slide it between those pink lips. I want to watch his eyes water as he chokes on me, those blue orbs on me the entire time.

"Are you okay?" Everly asks, leaning a little too close. "You're breathing really heavily and you're sweating."

I manage a small nod and then shake my head when the rest of my blood leaves my body and goes straight to my cock. It's going to explode.

"Shit," Everly says, and when the last student leaves the room he grabs my bag and wraps his arm around me, leading me toward my office. My dick is massive, so I pull my coat closed, making sure no one can see the giant zucchini in my pants.

I let him help me to my office, dipping my chin to my chest so people can't see that it's me he's cradling in his arms. And as soon as the door to my office closes behind me, Everly pushes me into my chair, grabs a bottle of water from my mini fridge, and hands it to me.

"Here, drink this. Are you having a heart attack?"

"Fuck you," I manage to snipe. "I'm not that old, and I'm very healthy. I eat leaves and seeds."

"Right," he says, still looking concerned and then my jacket splits open and his eyes settle on my throbbing dick.

"Oh," he says, nearly breathless.

I let out a small, pained whimper, and his eyes slash to mine.

"I'm fine. You should go," I manage to say, being very, very firm. He should not be here, kneeling in front of me, being every gay man's temptation. Especially if he's with Garrett. And more importantly, because he's my TA. He is off-limits.

Not that it stops my dick from jumping toward him.

"You look like you're in pain."

I am. I am in such pain. And it's all his fault.

"I'm fine," I murmur, and Everly's hands clutch the arms of my chair.

And then without warning, his face presses into my groin, a warm, deep pressure right against my dick. I can feel his cheek rubbing up against my hard length, and my entire body spasms. Oh shit. Oh fucking shit, I'm going to come if he does that again.

This is what I get for trying to be good, I think as I stare down at him, my eyes unblinking, my breath coming out in violent heaves. I'm practically wheezing, but Everly's face is on my dick and he's rubbing up against it, like a cat in heat, and it's making my balls draw up even further. Oh fuck me. They were already blue. All goddamn week they've been full and hard. And like a fool, I didn't do anything about it. I chose to ignore them and now I'm going to come in my pants. Again.

"Everly," I groan, and his big blue eyes flash up to meet mine as he parts his lips and mouths at my dick. It's over my pants, but still, the idea of it, the sight. It's all I need. My cock jerks, and I explode on a silent scream, my boxers filling with my release.

And the entire time, he mouths at me, almost as if he's trying to get a taste. He wants a taste of my cum.

Another spurt leaves me, and I bite down on my bottom lip so hard to contain the moan that bubbles up inside of me.

Everly inhales deeply, breathing me in and then licks a stripe along my zipper and over the emerging wet spot.

I shudder and then slump in my chair, my cock very happy and my mind very muddled.

"Hot," Everly says as he sits back on his heels and looks at me.

Our eyes meet, and the corner of his lip quirks up.

"You come so quickly," he says, almost in awe, and I feel myself blush.

Of course I do. I'm a sex-starved man in his thirties with a hot-as-fuck TA who sticks his face on my dick every chance he gets. Who wouldn't come quickly?

I manage to gather some of my wits. "I do not. That was just...a fluke."

His grin widens, and I frown at him.

"I think it's just you, Dr. Sinclair, and I love that. It's so sexy."

We stare at one another, my eyes settling on his blushing cheeks and his mussed hair before they slip down to the outline of his straining dick in his jeans.

He liked it. He liked it so much he's hard.

"I—I really need to clean up and you should leave," I say, not really wanting him to go but really needing to get a grip on the reality of this situation. I cannot have him doing this again. Especially in my place of work.

Everly shakes his head, pressing the heel of his palm to his dick. "I really don't wanna leave, not when I'm worried about your health."

I roll my eyes as best I can as I grab some tissues and start to clean myself up. Everly's eyes have fallen back to my crotch again, watching as I try my best to wipe away the evidence of my weakness. And that's what I am. I'm weak. So very weak for this guy. Never in my life have I behaved like this, so wanton, so impulsive.

And even when I know he has someone who likes him, someone who could even be his boyfriend for all I know.

"You do realize that this could be considered cheating?" I grumble, and Everly's eyes slash to mine.

"Yeah?"

"Yeah."

He worries his bottom lip, as if in thought, as if he's about to say something I probably don't want to hear. So, I shut it down before he can even begin.

"And besides that. I shouldn't have allowed it anyway. Because I have a date."

Everly's eyebrows fly upward. "A date?"

"Yes, a date."

"With who?"

"A very hot man," I lie and then toss the used tissues into the garbage can.

Everly's eyebrows lower and his mouth turns into a frown. Good. He should frown every once in a while. His smile is far too potent for the likes of me.

"And who is this very hot man?" he asks, and I sit up a little straighter, pressing down on my tie and trying to regain some composure. Sadly, my dick has other ideas. It just lives for my eternal embarrassment.

It's hard. Again.

Everly sees it too and points at it. "And just so you know, your dick doesn't want this other hot man. It wants me."

My mouth falls open, and I point at him. "Keep your voice down, Mr. Winslow."

Full Service

He rolls his eyes like a petulant teen and then stands up. "Fine. Then tell me. What's his name?"

I honestly can't remember it right now. Damn ribbon-man and his ridiculous name. And damn Everly for being so fucking hot that he's scrambled all of my neurons.

"You're lying. You don't have a date," Everly says with a laugh. "Fuck off, Dr. Sinclair."

I stand now too, wincing when I feel the stickiness still in my pants. I did a horrid job of cleaning myself up. I need to keep a fresh set of clothes in my office if Everly is going to continue to be my TA this semester. I can't go walking around with cum in my pants.

"I *do* have a date."

"Then tell me his name," he demands.

My fists clench, and I grind my teeth. "Fine. It's AlmondJoy."

Everly's mouth falls open, and he lets out a laugh. "Shut up. That's a total lie."

"It's not. That's his name."

I'm almost positive that's not his name, but I can't correct it. He's a candy bar now.

"You're lying," he says lowly, and I shake my head.

"I'm not. He's very eccentric. And he's my age. I'm sure we have a lot in common, and we're going to have so much fun."

Everly shakes his head and runs a hand through his hair. He looks a little unsure, and I despise it.

"And what does it matter anyways? You have that jock-guy wrapped around you all the time."

Everly freezes, his hand cupping the back of his neck. He really shouldn't stand like that. It's making his bicep pop out, and I want to sink my teeth into it.

"Right, I do have Garrett," he says and then his arm falls to his side with a sigh. Almost like he's given up. "Alright. You win. You have fun on your date. With *AlmondJoy*."

I nod and then walk to the door, realizing with horror that it wasn't locked. Anyone could have come in and seen Everly's face on my dick. Jesus Christ on a cracker.

"And you have fun on yours," I say, even though I hope that any date he goes on is horrible. Just absolutely wretched.

The two of us stare at each other, the door remaining shut. I should open it and push him out, but I don't. I just stare at him.

He's so fucking hot. God made no mistakes when he created him.

"Fine," he says, looking slightly defeated. "I will."

"You should."

Our eyes clash, and I suck in a breath, feeling my heartbeat triple just from how close he is.

And then without warning, Everly is on me, his lips crashing into mine, my back shoved up against the door with a small thump. His hands tangle in my hair, his tongue pressing into my mouth unbidden, and I let him. I let him kiss me. Let him devour my mouth as I clutch onto him for dear life.

Oh fuck. *Oh fuck.*

This is mind-melting, catastrophic, and I can't stop. I won't stop. I can feel his hard dick pressed against mine as he slashes his tongue in and out of my mouth, tangling with mine, warring with it. But the truth is, I'm not fighting this. Not at all. I'm just letting him plunder.

A soft whimper escapes me, and Everly lets out a low groan, his hips rocking up against my cock, making me shake.

There's no way I could come again. Absolutely no way.

Right?

I don't even know anymore. I can't even think. I just stand there and let him lick and nip and bite at my mouth. And when he pulls my tongue between his lips and sucks, I feel my knees start to wobble.

The kiss is frantic, heady, and erotic. I never want it to end, I want him to kiss me for all eternity. But before I can suggest it, he pulls away, my lips chasing his as he goes.

Everly's breathing heavily, his chest heaving as he grips my head in those strong hands. My lips feel swollen, and my entire body tingles from the pleasure of his mouth on mine.

"Right, Dr. Sinclair," he says and then his fingers fall from me and run through his hair, trembling slightly. "Oh fuck."

I swallow roughly, still tasting him on my tongue.

"Right. That's what I was going to say. Have fun on your date."

I can't even nod, I just stand there, blocking the exit. If I move, I'll fall over. I don't want to go on this date. Not anymore. Not when the hottest man on Earth just kissed me. I can't be expected to walk around with AlmondJoy now. There's no way. I'll be thinking of Everly the entire time.

"I should go," he says and points to the door, but I can't get my legs to work. They just wobble and shake. Everly seems to notice because he helps me slide to the side and props me up against the wall, his fingers lightly tracing over my swollen bottom lip before he sighs once more.

"Yeah, okay. I'm really gonna go now," he says, and I just blink at him.

He sucked all my words out of my throat. I can't find them. I may never speak again.

And just as they begin to bubble up, to ask him to kiss me again, to not leave, to break up with Garrett, bring me home and fuck me, he disappears out of my office. As if it never happened.

As if the kiss was just a figment of my imagination.

But it wasn't. It so wasn't.

The bruises on my lips suggest otherwise.

Cora Rose

He kissed me, and I can't forget it.

Chapter Ten

Silas

I don't know why I thought this date was a good idea. But I felt even more determined to go on it after Everly kissed me and then fled my office.

I've hyper-fixated on that kiss far more than I should. Far more than is healthy.

I made sure that LoveJoy—who is ironically not named after a candy bar after all—went out with me the very next day. Screw waiting for Saturday. We pushed it up to Thursday. Because I couldn't wait. I had to get this obsession with my TA under control.

And ribbon-man seemed like just the thing. He's so exotic and odd that I figured he'd be the perfect person to distract me from Everly.

I'm right about that, actually. The moment he shows up to the popular beachside restaurant in town, with its crowded tables and romantic low lights, I can see only him. It's hard to look away when he strides toward me, almost floating. Perhaps it's the brightly colored caftan dress he's wearing or the ribbons in his hair, but he looks positively ridiculous.

LoveJoy will certainly keep my mind off of Everly for the time being.

At least I hope so.

"Hello there," he says, leaning down, smelling of caramel. He presses a kiss to my cheek, and I allow it. Not that it feels anything like Everly's lips on my skin, but that's not why I'm here. I'm here to forget about that man and find someone to have fun with.

I nod and smooth my tie down. "Hello."

He grins at me and then sits down in the chair opposite me.

"I'm glad you found the place okay."

"I am too," I reply, surprised that this restaurant is somewhat normal. I expected something very offbeat and strange. But then again, something weird could happen. With LoveJoy you never know.

"Howdy, partners. I'm Adam," the waiter says, swinging by and handing us menus. He hands them to us upside down, and I glance up at him, noticing that he's sucking on his lips a little too vigorously. Hm.

"Howdy right back," LoveJoy replies. The waiter, Adam, eyes LoveJoy and his caftan a little too long. Probably because it shimmers brightly despite the dim lighting.

"Nice robe, man," Adam says. "It's very sparkly. Kind of moves too when you squint your eyeballs."

LoveJoy preens under the attention. I'm wondering what substance our waiter is on. Nothing good, I assume.

"Could we order drinks now?" I ask, distracting the waiter, who is reaching out and fiddling with the ribbons in LoveJoy's hair. It's fine by me, but honestly, I just want to get this date over with. And the longer the waiter fiddles with LoveJoy's hair, the longer I have to sit here and pretend I'm not thinking about Everly.

"Right on. What can I get you?" Adam asks, and I sigh, ordering a water with lemon—I need to keep my wits about me—and LoveJoy orders a porn star martini. I don't even want to know what that is. If LoveJoy strips down to drink it, I honestly wouldn't be surprised.

This is what I get for agreeing to a date with him.

"So," I say, trying to make conversation once the waiter finally leaves. I'll do just about anything to make this move a little quicker. "You have an interesting name."

"Oh, you don't even know the half of it," he says, flitting his hands around. "I hated it growing up, got teased a lot, but now I own it. LoveJoy Dracula Smith."

A snort escapes me. "Dracula?"

"I know. My mother is a wild hippie and my dad is a dreary, grumpy accountant who hates the outdoors. I think they compromised."

"Do you have any siblings?" I ask, wondering what their names could be.

"Of course. Two sisters. GracieDoll and BloomCloud."

I stare at him. The first sounds like a creepy, murderous Muppet and the second sounds like an atomic bomb.

He shrugs. "I know. I *know*. And you don't even want to know their middle names."

I lean forward. "Actually, yes, I do."

I can't help but be interested in this. I may want this date to be over with, but I *am* distracted. Yes, this was the perfect decision. LoveJoy is making me *not* think of Everly. Even though I just did. But whatever. I can't expect perfection right off the bat.

"Well, Gracie's middle name is Chaos and Bloom's is Ozul."

I can't help but smile at that. My god, this family. No

wonder LoveJoy wanders around in ribbons. He can't help himself with how he was raised.

"I also have a cousin named Basil, if that helps. And another named Aspen."

"Hm, sounds like your family is quite...fun."

"They are. No one like them."

"And this ribbon dance? Is this something your mother taught you?" I ask.

"No, it's something I created while high in the woods. I really did enjoy it and thought I'd spread the love and joy I felt that night to others. To live up to my name."

I can't tell if he's joking or not. But then again, I could imagine him out in the woods, flapping those ribbons around and speaking to the birds.

"So, what were you high on?" I ask, genuinely curious.

"Oh, Ayahuasca. It's a South American brew that causes hallucinations. Or so I was told."

I stare at him as the waiter brings over his porn drink and my water with a cucumber in it. No lemon to be seen.

And I didn't even have a chance to look at the menu. LoveJoy is making my head spin and not in a good way.

"Do you do drugs?" LoveJoy asks, and I nearly choke on my water.

"No, I do not."

The waiter pipes up at that moment, "Drugs? Hell yes. I do. I'm on 'shrooms at the moment, but don't tell my boss."

I glower at him as LoveJoy flutters a ribbon around the man's face. "Be blessed!"

Oh, for fuck's sake, I think as I stare down at my menu. I should order quickly before the waiter passes out behind the counter and forgets all about us.

"Let me know when you're ready to order, I'm going to go talk to the wall," the waiter says. "It tells me funny jokes."

Full Service

"Jesus," I murmur as LoveJoy just nods. Apparently he understands wall speak. I let out a shuddering breath, searching like hell for anything that looks appetizing and settle on a salad.

Such fun.

LoveJoy, of course, orders about ten dishes, and I wonder who's paying for this. Probably me. I doubt he gets paid all that much to flutter ribbons around and grind on walkers. But who knows? Maybe he's a millionaire. Maybe his ribbon skills are much desired.

A small snort escapes me. Of course they would be. Who wouldn't want LoveJoy fluttering around you like a pigeon.

"I apologize for my gluttonous behavior," LoveJoy says when the waiter ambles away. "But I am ravenous."

"No problem," I say, wondering where he's going to put all that food. He's not big by any means.

"And the portions here are so small. So don't be surprised if you're hungry after your salad."

And he's right, when my salad is finally placed in front of me, it's about the size of my thumb.

I stare at it and blink. Am I hallucinating? Maybe someone put drugs in my cucumber water.

"I would share my food with you, but I get a little feral when it comes to being hungry," LoveJoy explains, his ten plates set nicely around him. He has enough food for an average-sized meal.

He obviously should have warned me that they feed you like rabbits here.

I watch as he eats and then look down at my salad once more. *This is my life now*, I think as I shove the entire single leaf into my mouth all at once.

As I chew, I sigh. This blows a big one. I know I'll be hungry right after this, but I refuse to order more because it's so damn expensive. This leaf was at least twenty dollars. And I don't even think I taste dressing on it.

Suddenly, my mind is thrown to Everly and how he teased me over my food choices when we went to grab dinner. How he ribbed me endlessly for being an old man.

Fuck, I'd much rather be here with him, watching him eat, watching that throat bob up and down as he swallows.

I shift in my seat and take a sip of my water, hoping it fills me up enough until I can get home and microwave a meal. I'll sit with my fish and watch as she poops.

Such a lucky guy I am.

Out of the corner of my eye, a familiar figure makes its way inside, and I freeze, the cool rim of my cup settled against my lips.

Everly is *here*.

My eyes swivel to the right and see that he's not alone. He's with that hot jock, Garrett.

Our eyes meet and Everly lifts his lips in a small, smug smile. He's here with that gorgeous specimen, and I'm stuck with a shiny, fluttering ribbon.

For fuck's sake.

How embarrassing.

"What are you looking at?" LoveJoy asks, his cheeks bulging with food, and I immediately feel a bit guilty because he seems like a perfectly nice person.

"Nothing," I mumble even though it's something. He's something. Something I can't have, obviously. Because he's my TA and I'm a professor with a slightly vague code of conduct to follow.

Right?

"Are you sure you don't want to order something else? You really didn't get much," LoveJoy says, and I shake my head, watching from the corner of my eye as Everly and Garrett take a seat. Right next to us.

Horrible customer service. Despicable people, really.

They should know better.

I glance over at Everly, who is sitting directly next to me and watch as he grins at me. "Hello, Dr. Sinclair. Fancy seeing you here."

He turns his gaze to LoveJoy, who waggles a ribbon at him.

"Are you on a date?" Everly asks, looking smug.

"Indeed," I grumble and then turn my gaze to Garrett. "As are you, it seems."

Everly's grin widens. "So it seems."

Garrett reaches his hand out toward me, a big, beefy hand to go along with his big beefy muscles. I reluctantly shake it, and so does LoveJoy, his cheeks turning a pretty pink.

"Love the dress, dude," Garrett tells him, and I watch as LoveJoy turns positively red.

"Thank you."

"Garrett," he says and LoveJoy takes a sip of his drink, smacking his lips together slightly.

"LoveJoy."

"Cool name," Garrett says with a smile.

"Thank you. Yours is nice too."

Everly and I watch the exchange and part of me wonders if we should leave them to it. The way LoveJoy is blushing and the way that Garrett is eyeing LoveJoy's caftan like he wants to crawl inside it is making me feel a little less guilty for not being into this date.

Perhaps LoveJoy can find someone who enjoys his ribbons. Maybe Garrett is that guy.

"The portions are *very* small," I tell Everly while Garrett and LoveJoy continue to chat. "And our waiter is high on drugs."

Everly chuckles and runs a hand over his mouth. "Let me guess. You got a salad."

"More like a leaf, but yes."

"And what kind of drugs is he on? Should we ask for a hit?"

"Fuck no," I murmur as LoveJoy takes a ribbon from his pocket and waves it around his head. Garrett claps his hands and guffaws loudly, drawing the stares of other patrons.

Oh, for shit's sake. This is a disaster. This was supposed to be an outing to rid myself of Everly once and for all, but here he is, right next to me, looking delectable.

He holds up his menu and squints his eyes. "Kinda pricey for a leaf," he says and glances over at me.

I roll my eyes.

"I had to take money from my retirement to afford that leaf, thank you very much."

Everly's eyes go to the plates surrounding LoveJoy.

"Seems you need to pay for his meals too. Since it's a date and all."

I glower at him, my eyes narrowed and shooting laser beams his way. Very unsexy laser beams, that will most definitely not sear his clothes right off him.

"Seems you may be working as a professor far longer than you expected," Everly adds, and I purse my lips in frustration.

He's right. I will have to with the way LoveJoy is putting down his meal. If he orders dessert, I'll die still teaching, my arthritic old body collapsing in front of a sea of students.

That makes my lips soften and quirk up. How morbidly funny.

"You know what," LoveJoy says and then stands up. "Let's scoot our tables together."

"Fuck yeah. Great idea, man. Plus, you smell hella good."

I stare at Garrett, who doesn't seem to acknowledge me. Or really notice I'm here. He shook my hand but then promptly forgot I existed. Which is fine by me. He can have LoveJoy.

I watch as Garrett stands up to help move the tables together, leaving me sitting in my chair in the middle of the room.

The waiter comes back, his pupils blown wide and blinks at us. "Is it me, or did the tables move?"

I sigh and stand, moving my chair right next to Everly.

Everly, who smells ridiculously manly and who's leg drifts over and presses against mine.

I should not allow this. Not at all.

There is a thirteen percent chance I will stop this.

"It's not you, mushroom-man," I say. "We moved them together."

Adam nods and runs a hand over his face in relief. "Thank fuck. The walls were scaring me, man. They're not funny anymore."

I let out a small laugh but it's cut off when I feel Everly's hand slip under the tablecloth and land on my thigh. I feel his touch right up my balls. If I come again, untouched, I will never live it down. I'll have to hand my penis over to the authorities for a crime.

A crime against my manhood.

"You should not be touching me," I grumble lowly, not wanting LoveJoy to hear. Not that he's listening. He's turned his body completely toward Garrett and is ignoring me completely.

"Should I stop?" Everly asks, his hand traveling a little further up my leg. I feel his touch through my clothes, feel the way it sears my skin and sets me on fire.

"You most definitely should?" It comes out as a question, and I see Everly's lips twitch.

"Seems you don't know what you want."

Oh, but I do. I know what I want, but I can't have it. Right?

I nod my head and then shake it, unsure of what he said. I can't think clearly when his fingers are digging into my thigh like that.

I glance over at LoveJoy for help, but he's not paying me any mind. Neither is Garrett. I'm pretty sure I could pay for dinner and leave and they wouldn't be any the wiser.

"Why are you here anyways?" I ask, finally getting my brain to work.

"Looked like a fun place to eat," Everly says, and I shift in my seat, resulting in Everly's hand scooting up my leg. He's almost brushing my crotch, and we all know how that will end.

"It looks like you came here to interfere with my date."

"With AlmondJoy?" Everly asks as his fingers graze my traitorously hard dick. Damnable thing. Won't go down for a second when he's in the room. Or anywhere on Earth apparently. Seems I may need to move to the moon to escape this silly obsession.

"I admit, he is very pretty."

I scoff when I see LoveJoy stand up and flitter his hands around, the ribbons dancing around him rhythmically. Must be some kind of magic he employs to get them to do that. And Garrett is eating it up. He's grinning and cheering, his eyes never leaving that man.

"Seems like your date likes him just fine as well."

Everly's thumb swirls around the tip of my dick, and I let out a low groan. I should really move away. Instead, I arch my hips up, searching for more.

"Wanna know the truth?" he asks, leaning closer, his lips brushing my earlobe. Just that touch sends me toward the edge of bliss. "I couldn't give a fuck."

Oh god, I think as I feel his hand drag down my dick. I want to unzip my pants, push him onto the ground, and stuff my cock right down his throat.

But of course, that would land us in jail.

And there's no way I'd survive in a place like that.

Just as I open my mouth to respond, LoveJoy flips his leg dramatically up into the air. How he gets it perpendicular to the ceiling I'll never know, but his flexibility is astounding. He also manages to show everyone in the vicinity his panties, but that's not the only issue. On the way down, he knocks his heel into a serving tray, sending plates of food flying.

LoveJoy gasps, Garrett claps loudly, and Everly takes his shot, his fingers wrapping around my dick in a spectacular squeeze.

It's enough to set me off.

I groan loudly as I lean forward, feeling my cock pulse. Oh my god, if he does that again, I'm going to come.

I can't handle him. He's potent.

"Oh my god, I'm so sorry!" LoveJoy says just as our waiter appears and drops and rolls around in the food splattered on the floor. "I didn't mean to do that. I'm a peacemaker!"

"The world is ending!" the waiter suddenly shouts. "The aliens have come!"

Everly is chuckling, and I just sit there, mouth agape. Mostly because Everly hasn't let up on rubbing my dick and I'm staving off an orgasm as we speak.

This is life or death it seems.

"I'll pay for this. I promise," LoveJoy is saying, his cheeks flushed red.

Garrett grins at him and then pulls him into his lap, nuzzling his face into LoveJoy's neck. Suffice it to say, this date has gone terribly. It has done nothing to distract me from Everly. It only seemed to bring him closer.

To my dick.

"We could go," Everly says softly, his lips brushing my ear once more.

Cora Rose

I stare at the mess, at the waiter being hauled up by his manager, and find some words.

"Yeah, we should go. Let me pay."

With shaking hands, I pull out several hundred-dollar bills and set them on the table. That should be enough to cover it all. I'm pretty sure I'm overpaying, but at the same time, we did make a huge mess. It's only fair.

"Look at you, Mr. Money Man," Everly says with a grin. "Do you always carry hundred-dollar bills around with you?"

"For emergencies." I glance around. "And this is definitely one."

His hand squeezes my dick once more, and I gasp, flicking his hand away, needing to get out of here before I walk out with a wet spot on the front of my slacks.

"Can I get a ride home?" Everly asks when he stands up and follows me to the restaurant door, not even saying goodbye to Garrett.

To be fair, I didn't say anything to LoveJoy either. But he was in Garrett's lap and didn't seem to notice me. Which is fine by me. I don't need to be dating a man who does the can-can in the middle of a restaurant. That's not my scene or my preference.

"Fine, but no more funny business," I say sternly, and Everly places a hand over his heart.

"Only the funniest of business, I promise."

I scowl. That's not what I said. Not at all. But I still let him follow me to my car and open the door for him. Like the gentleman I am.

I will behave like a gentleman the rest of the night.

I will.

Chapter Eleven

Everly

I somehow manage to persuade Dr. Sinclair to take me back to his place. I don't know how I did it, but I did. Seems the full moon is working its magic tonight. I just suggested it and he did an illegal U-turn and drove me right to his place.

"No funny business," he says again.

I bite my bottom lip to keep my smile at bay. Right, no funny business. None at all.

Because being with him won't be funny at all. No, it will be mind-blowing.

Hot as fuck.

I don't know what it is about this guy, but I am totally obsessed. Showing up to his date was next-level stalker shit, but I did it anyways.

Didn't help that Garrett encouraged it. He's a terrible influence.

But it went better than expected. Not only did the date go horribly, but I got to touch his dick.

I want to touch it again.

Not that he lets me.

He sweeps inside his townhouse, introduces me to his fish, and then disappears into his room.

"Make yourself at home," he says, and I honestly feel like I should strip out of my clothes and sit naked on the couch.

I contemplate it for a moment. A long moment. Would that be too manipulative?

Probably, but then again, like Dr. Sinclair said, my brain isn't fully developed. If I make a bad decision, we can just blame it on my underdeveloped brain.

But before I can strip naked and lay myself on the couch like a fifties porn star, he reappears, his tie gone and the top two buttons of his shirt undone. Well, hell. Now I'm even hornier. I can see his chest hair.

I want to rub my face in it.

"What are you doing?" he asks as I stare at him, drooling. I force my gaze up to his eyes, and I make myself behave.

Well, mostly behave. I do whip my shirt off and watch as he sputters and chokes.

I do have a nice chest, if I do say so myself.

I constrict my abs, and he wheezes.

"Put your damn shirt back on, Mr. Winslow."

Oh god, when he calls me that... It's unhelpful and doesn't make me want to put my shirt back on. No siree.

It makes me want to get even more naked.

"No thanks," I say and then grin at him. "It's getting hot in here."

"Oh, for fuck's sake," he says, even though his dick is hardening in his pants. I can see the outline through his pressed slacks. I want to rub my face against it again and feel it pump its release against me.

Full Service

"I will throw you out on your ass, young man," he says, his voice raspy.

I just stare at him and start to unbutton my pants. When he talks like a strict teacher, I get all hot and bothered.

"Keep going," I say as I slide my zipper down.

Dr. Sinclair sputters, and his cheeks redden. "Keep your pants on."

"Fuck off. Not when you're going all dirty professor on me."

He gapes at me as I kick my shoes and pants to the side, leaving me clad in only my boxers. I know I said we would keep this professional, but that ended the moment he stuck his face in my ass and licked my hole.

There's no going back now.

"Put your clothes back on," he says, even though his own fingers are unbuttoning his shirt and showing me that magnificent chest.

I grab on to my dick as he pulls it open, and I feel my balls draw up. I've never in my life been so obsessed with a guy. There have been a few flings here and there that did it for me, but nothing like this man.

Dr. Sinclair is in a league all his own.

"Fuck yes. Take it all off," I say, sounding like the people who stand in the crowd while I'm stripping off my clothes. This is what this man has reduced me to.

The minute he sat in my chair and I watched him come untouched, just from a shake of my ass, I knew I was a goner.

"I'm not taking off a thing," he says as he tosses his shirt aside. I take in the dark hair on his chest, the way his waist tapers down into narrow hips, the dip of his belly button. And then my eyes settle on a sleeve of tattoos lining his forearm.

Oh hell, why is that so hot? Of course he has secret tattoos under all that buttoned-up goodness.

I let out a low groan, and Dr. Sinclair reaches between his legs and cups his cock.

I want to sink to my knees and rub on him, mark him like some animal, but I stay where I am. I think if I approach, he'll call the whole damn thing off.

"Please. Take it off. Take it off," I beg as I reach my hand into my boxers and start to stroke my leaking length. Dr. Sinclair is watching me, his eyes nearly black, his cheeks bright red.

I want him on top of me. I want him to *grind*.

"I'll be so good," I say. "I'll stay over here. Just show me. I want to see it all."

He lets out a shaky breath but hesitates long enough to let me know that he's thinking about it. And I know that I've hooked him when I hear his zipper slide down and watch as his thumbs hook into his waistband of his pants and slowly peel them off.

"Fine. Just this once and then never again."

"Fuck yes," I murmur.

"You stay over there. No touching."

"I promise," I say as I eagerly shuck my boxers, kicking them onto an end table.

Dr. Sinclair eyes the fabric as it dangles but makes no move to extricate it. Instead, he just peels his underwear off and kicks them to the side, showing me everything.

And all of it is so damn good.

I know he's older than me, but his body is so fucking hot. His cock is too. And don't get me started on those balls. They hang there between his legs, ripe and ready for my mouth.

Not that I'll go over there and suck on them.

I'll behave. I'll so behave.

I grip my dick and give it a solid pump, watching as Dr. Sinclair does the same thing, his movements in time with my own.

"Fuck yes. Squeeze harder," I say and watch as Dr. Sinclair's knuckles turn white. He's strangling his dick. So I do the same. It's only fair.

"You're so hot. So hot," I whisper, and Dr. Sinclair's nostrils flare.

"Stop lying."

"I'm not," I whine as I arch my hips up. "You're so hot. I want to touch you. I want to kiss you again."

Dr. Sinclair groans and shakes his head, his feet shuffling a little closer to me. He's now only half a room away.

"Come here. *Come here.* Break the rules. Break them with me," I taunt as my fist shuttles up and down my shaft.

I can see his resolution breaking, can see him warring with himself. I want him to push me down on the sofa, spread my legs, and take me. But before he can, before he even moves, I hear a splash behind me and I watch as his fish throws itself out of its tank.

I gasp and so does Dr. Sinclair. Then he's rushing past me, scooping up the flapping fish and placing it back in the water.

"She tried to kill herself!" he says, his eyes wide. "She's never done that before."

"Probably didn't want to see us jacking off."

"Jesus, why did she do that? Is she unhappy? I just cleaned her tank last week!"

I glance over at him, our naked bodies crouched down on the floor, his eyes round with worry.

"I honestly don't know. That was weird as fuck, but look, she's happy now. She's under that coral. Is she smiling?"

Dr. Sinclair glances up and then sighs. "Do you really think she was just mortified by what she saw? Usually, I go into my bedroom and use my toys..."

His words trail off as I stare at him, my dick bobbing between my legs.

"Toys?" I ask lowly.

He swallows, gulping loudly.

"Perhaps."

"Show me," I rasp, unable to control myself. I need to see this or I may die.

"Absolutely not," he says, even though he stands, placing his cock right near my mouth.

I should open up wide and swallow him. But I behave like I said I would. I watch as he turns on his heel, and I stand on wobbly legs as I follow him down the small hallway to his room.

"I need to wash my hands. Fish juice doesn't belong on my dick."

I couldn't care less about that. I'd take his fish dicks any day.

When he's done, we stand there in the dark, both of our chests heaving, our cocks hard and leaking. I won't make the first move, but I sure as hell can prod.

"Come on. Show me," I tell him, and he lets out a small whimper, a small assent. He wants this just as much as me.

He doth protest too much.

"I have quite a few to choose from."

I squeeze my dick in excitement. "Show me all of them."

Dr. Sinclair seems unsure, almost like he wants to say no, but then he moves toward the bedstand and pulls open a drawer.

And I see it. I see it *all*.

So many toys, so many possibilities.

"This doesn't mean that I'm going to use them while you watch."

"How about *I* use them on you while *you* watch," I say, and Dr. Sinclair rolls his eyes, even though I can see the flush on his cheeks.

He likes that idea.

A lot.

Full Service

"Absolutely not," he says, as he lies down on the bed, his legs spread, his hand grabbing the lube.

I move toward him, picking out a dildo from the drawer. A big one. Probably as big as me. I want to watch as it slides inside of him, want to imagine that it's me who's doing the fucking.

"This is breaking all sorts of rules," he says as he squirts some lube onto his fingers and reaches between his legs. "We absolutely must stop."

I kneel on the bed, watching as his fingers push inside of him, opening himself for me.

"Fuck yes," I say as I stroke my dick. This is the hottest thing I've ever seen.

I want more. I want to see it all.

"You should turn around and not watch," he says as he pushes another finger inside of himself.

I huff a small laugh, his little protestations won't work on me. I get why he's saying them, plausible deniability, but I swear I wouldn't turn my back on this if it could save my life.

No, I'd die trying to see him stuff himself full.

And I'd die a happy man.

"Mr. Winslow," he grunts and then arches his hips up, his cock spurting precum from the tip. I watch it leak, wetting my lips. I want to fall on it, want to suck him into the back of my throat, want to hear him come again.

"Everly, call me Everly, Dr. Sinclair," I say and I watch as his eyes settle on me, three fingers up his ass, the other squeezing his cock.

"Then you have to call me Silas."

I nod, loving the sound of that. What a sexy name. "Okay then, *Silas*, show me what you got."

I set the dildo down next to him and he picks it up. It's long and thick, perfect for fucking. And he must think so too because a second later, his fingers have slipped from his hole and the tip of the silicone cock is entering it.

He doesn't move slow, doesn't inch it inside. No, he shoves it up there with a gasp, my name leaving his lips a moment later.

Fuck, hearing him moan that, it's scorching my skin, my self-control already teetering on the edge.

If he does that again, I'll fall on him and fuck him myself.

Silas pushes the dildo further into him, until just the base is visible and he swivels it, making low, tortured gasps as he does it. It's too hot, too fucking sexy.

I can't keep myself under control. I'm a stretched elastic, close to snapping.

"Everly," he says as he pulls it out and then shoves it back in. "*Everly.*"

"Fuck, fuck," I pant and then I'm on him, my mouth covering his cock and sucking it to the back of my throat. Silas cries out, his back arching off the bed as I grab the dildo and rock it into his needy hole.

Two sucks in and he explodes, his eyes screwed shut, his mouth open in a scream.

I swallow it all, tasting him on my lips. And when he finally comes down from the high of his orgasm, I pull out the dildo and pump my dick with my fist, splashing my release across his hole, his balls, and his cock.

Silas watches the entire thing, his eyes stormy and dark.

And then I fall forward, pressing myself against him. I don't even care that my mess is smearing against our skin. All I want to do is kiss him. Again.

My lips trail across his scruffy jaw and when they land on his lips, he sighs, his fingers curling into my hair and tugging.

Our tongues tangle, our mouths slanted over each other. It's languid and lazy, and when we finally pull apart, my lips feel swollen.

"That was real nice," I say with a small smile, watching as Silas's eyelids flutter open.

"That's one word for it. I'd probably go with shocking."

"Shocking that you couldn't turn me down?" I tease, and Silas rolls his eyes.

"I did turn you down, over and over, but you were relentless. I'm entirely blameless."

I scoot a little closer to him, my hands trailing across his skin, feeling my cum smear into it.

"I think you caved quite easily," I tell him. "Really easily, if I remember correctly."

He scoffs and then sits up, his tattooed arm moving up to his chest and scratching. I want to know what those tattoos represent, what they mean, but before I can ask about them, he stands up.

"This was a mistake," he grumbles, and I scramble after him, following him into the en suite bathroom.

"I mean, you're using that word far too liberally."

He glowers at me in the mirror and then softens into me when my hands slide across his stomach.

"I'm going to bring you home, like I should have after dinner."

"But we haven't technically had dinner. And I'm hungry."

It's the truth. I could eat. His cum only filled me up a little bit. Although, I could go for round two. And three. I could suck his dick all night long.

Not that he plans to let me.

His hands peel mine off his chest and he steps away from me, looking dour.

"We can pick something up before I drop you off."

I sigh, watching as he grabs a washcloth and hands it to me.

"You want to clean up?"

I don't want to. I want to walk around all night with

evidence of this on my skin, but I do as he says because he looks so grumpy about it. I would be too if I turned down the possibility of sex all night long. Because let me tell you, I'm willing and ready.

But I get why he's putting up a fight. This is his job on the line, and he's risking a lot by even entertaining this. Maybe I should quit, but then I think of my bills, of my sunken ceiling caving in precariously after the rainstorm and sigh.

I really can't afford to live anywhere else at the moment.

And my landlord is probably a criminal. There's no way any of the issues we've brought to him will get fixed.

"Alright, I'm ready," I say when I pull my pants back on.

I'm rebelling slightly, putting up a bit of a stink. I don't put my shirt on. I refuse. And I leave my pants unzipped and unbuttoned, so Silas is forced to look at me.

"Put on your fucking clothes," he grumbles, and I shake my head.

"I don't feel like it."

I grin smugly and his eyes narrow. He knows what I'm trying to do. I won't get away with this.

"At least zip up your pants."

"No thanks. My dick is getting hard again. I want to let it have some breathing room."

His eye twitches, and I feel my lips turn up.

"Really, I can't suffocate it or else it gets claustrophobic."

He pinches the bridge of his nose, and if it were anyone else, I'd push into him, press my lips to his skin, and make him forget all his annoyance. But this is different. He is different. Not only is he older than me, more mature, but he's also technically my boss. Which puts a damper on things, a real dip in the road.

"I'll bring you home, claustrophobic dick and all," he says and then tosses me a sweatshirt from the closet nearest the door.

Full Service

It lands on my chest, and I can't help but pull it toward my nose and inhale.

Fuck, it smells like him.

This is the only reason I'm putting it on. I want to wear him.

There's a very good chance that I'll forget to give this back to him.

More like a one hundred percent chance.

"This way," he says as he leads me to his car.

I want to refuse, to chain myself to his door, but feel like that might be toeing the line of insane. And while I don't mind a little light craziness when pursuing someone, I feel like that would just be full-on creepy.

And I want to come off as sexy. Not a serial killer.

I slide into his car and shut the door, pulling the sweatshirt up slightly and sniffing the fabric.

"Put your address in here," he says, his voice curt. He points to his phone, and I press my address into it.

"You want me to snap you a dick pic, just in case you want it later?"

He sputters slightly, his cheeks flushed red.

"Fuck no. I do not want that."

"You sure?" I tease.

He stares at me and wets his lips.

"I'll be right back," he says and then gets out of the car, leaving me alone with his phone.

I'm almost positive he left so I could get in some nice shots of my dick.

So I do. I take as many as I can before he returns. And when he does, I hand the phone over, trying to look innocent, but looking more like an eager dog.

Woof. Woof.

"Why are you breathing like that?" he asks, his eyebrows meeting. "You didn't do something naughty, did you?"

Oh yes, I was very, *very* bad, but I just shrug like the innocent man I'm not.

I hope he looks at those pictures as soon as he gets home. I want to know that my cock is the last thing he sees before he goes to sleep. I want him to count my cocks like sheep.

"Alright, well, I'll have to check very thoroughly later, to make sure nothing bad is on here."

I turn my gaze to the window and smile.

Oh, there are some very naughty things on there, but I won't say a word about it and neither will he. I hope he keeps them forever. I hope that he looks at them ten years from now and remembers me.

For some reason that thought bothers me more than it should, but I shake it off. Silas is driving me home. This thing between us, these shenanigans, are nothing serious. It's just a little messing around with the hottie professor.

Nothing more.

I stare at the wet streets as he drives me across town, the tires splashing through puddles as we go. Our places aren't far from one another, but they're not close enough to walk. Shame. If I was close enough to walk to his place, I'd be in his bushes, peering through the window like the creeper I've become.

I'd fog up the glass, my nose pressed right against the cool panes as I rub one out.

Never thought another person would reduce me to this, but here I am.

Dr. Sinclair does it for me. Big time.

They should write a romance novel about us.

When he finally pulls up to my crumbling place, even in the dark I'm a little embarrassed by my living conditions. But then I see one of my roommates, Murphy, out on the curb, a box in his beefy hands.

Full Service

I pause a moment before rolling my window down. "Yo, Murph, what's that?"

"Ah, fuck man, there you are. Been trying to get a hold of you. The roof caved in on me right when I was taking a shit! It's a mess in there, a real biohazard."

I stare at him, feeling myself heat in embarrassment. I can't believe it finally happened. It was sagging after those rainstorms we had, like a pregnant woman about to give birth, but I really tried not to think about it.

I really tried to stay optimistic.

I was manifesting only good things as the plaster strained under the force of the water.

"Why in God's name is your roof caving in?" Silas asks gruffly, and I turn toward him, feeling my cheeks heat.

"I'm pretty sure our landlord is a slumlord and he's been neglecting the place for a while. The ceiling's been sagging since we moved in and the water finally broke it."

"Unacceptable," he grumbles.

"Yeah, well, it's all I can afford." I run my hand through my hair and then sigh. There's nothing to be done about it now. Just onward and upward, my best foot forward. Like always. "Anyways. Thanks for the ride."

I step out, meeting Murphy where he's standing. "So, like, how bad is it really? Can we stay there still?"

"Fuck no. Everything is wet and the landlord said we can't move back in, not until it's fixed."

"Well, what the hell are we supposed to do then?"

"Um, well, I'm going to go stay with my girlfriend, and Meena is going to live in a tent."

"What the hell?" I ask with a laugh. "A tent?"

"Yeah, apparently it's real nice. I could have her shoot you a link if you want to look at that as an option."

"Yeah, please do," I joke, just as I hear a rumble from behind me.

Silas.

"You're not living in a goddamn tent," he grunts and then comes to stand near me. His hand brushes my own and that small touch sends tendrils of pleasure shooting up my arm.

"Do you have a better idea?" I ask him. "I don't have any other options."

Silas purses his lips, his hand fiddling with the top button of his shirt.

"You do. Of course you do."

I arch an eyebrow. "Care to share with the class because I'm at a loss."

"Your dad."

"No, he lives in a trailer. Travels for work. It's not an option."

Silas eyes me, his eyebrows meeting.

"Fine. With me. You can stay with me."

A snort slips out of my nose. I sound like a pig in heat.

"I can't stay with you," I say and then lower my voice. "Do you know how tempting that would be?" I swear, he must have no idea. I'd be humping him all fucking day long. My dick would be chafed from how much I'd be jacking it.

His eye twitches and then he clears his throat. "Yes, well, we can figure that out later. There's no way you're sleeping in a tent. Good fuck."

"Yes, good fuck," I murmur. A good fuck with him would be very nice.

Silas sighs and then motions to the apartment building. "Can you at least go in and grab your things?"

I shout over to Murph, asking him that question, and he nods.

"Yeah, you can go in. Just be careful. May end up going through the floor."

"You are *not* going in there," Silas says behind me, but I can't just leave my shit in the apartment. I have my coursework in there.

"Yeah, well, I have to."

He grumbles and follows me, nearly clipping my heels as we go. I kind of like that he's following me. Normally, anyone doing this would put me off, but for some reason, with grumpy Dr. Sinclair it really gets me going. I love it.

We make it to the elevator, and I press the button. I hear a very disheartening clang inside the elevator shaft, and then Silas huffs behind me.

"We are not taking that death box. Where are the stairs?"

"Listen, old man, I don't think your knees can handle those."

I grin at him and he takes a step forward, making my cock twitch in my pants. Oh, he looks so delicious right now.

"I'll show you just how good my knees are when we get back home."

Welp, there goes my twitching cock right up to full-mast. It can sail the ocean blue at this point.

"Please do," I say as I lead him toward the stairs. "I feel like I really need you to prove this hypothesis."

"I'll prove it alright," he tells me as I start to jog up the stairs. He keeps up with me, even if I do hear his knees cracking every once in a while. Just means they're well used.

Hopefully they are even more so when I get back to his place.

I can't believe I'm even entertaining this. That he is. For fuck's sake, this is going to end terribly, but I'm too enamored to turn him down.

Just think of all the things we could do together. I could

wander around naked and tempt him to take his clothes off. I could cockwarm him on the sofa while we watch TV.

Well, maybe not. The fish might not like that.

Better to cockwarm him in bed after eating his ass.

The thought makes me take the stairs two at a time, and by the time we make it to my fifth-floor apartment, Silas is hunched over, his hands on his thighs.

"You okay there?" I ask, and he stares up at me. A piece of his hair flops onto his forehead and his lips purse. He looks like he's about to give me a kiss.

I like that look a little too much.

"I'm perfectly fine. Just haven't walked up any stairs recently."

"Is that so?"

"Yes, that's so. Not this many anyways. I didn't realize you lived on the top floor."

"Yep, the one and only. Hence the caved-in ceiling. And the many other things that have gone wrong with this place."

Dr. Sinclair straightens and he looks very much like a Silas at the moment, a little disheveled and sweaty. Kind of like when he was ramming that dildo up his ass earlier.

I adjust my hard cock and his eyes swivel down to it. He wets his lips. Hungry.

He wants to show me just how well those knees work right at this very moment.

But he seems to have other plans. He runs a hand through his hair and arches a very meticulous eyebrow. Is that a thing? Can eyebrows be meticulous?

I'll have to research this, for science.

"What other issues have you been having in this hell hole?" he asks, his eyes turning toward the peeling paint on the walls.

"Uh, you know, the usual. Caved-in ceiling, wet floors, leaky faucets, the smell of rotting corpse."

His eyes widen. "None of that is usual, Everly. I think this place should be burned to the ground. Rotting corpse?"

"Well, who knows? There could be someone buried between the walls."

"Oh, for fuck's sake, Everly. Absolutely not."

He grabs on to my hand and leads me forward. Not that he knows where he's going. But it sure is damn cute.

"Over here," I say, as I lead him to a door with caution tape strewn on it.

"Seems just like a crime scene," he grumbles and then pushes his way in. The door swings open easily, and I swear Silas is going to have a stroke right here and now.

"Oh yeah, and the lock doesn't work."

He sighs and makes his way inside, his feet squishing on the floor.

It's pretty bad, worse than I imagined. There is insulation on the ground and part of the ceiling just lying there. The entire space smells like mold, and I wonder what my room looks like.

We trudge through the mess, and I manage a small squeak when I see the state of my room I shared with Murphy. It's terrible. Our beds are wrecked, wet the entire way through, there's no ceiling, and I'm pretty sure that someone rummaged through my dresser drawer. The cash I had stashed there is completely gone.

I rub at my tired eyes, and for the first time since arriving, I realize how bad this really is.

This is so damn bad.

"Get what you can, Everly," Silas says softly, his hand moving to my lower back and pushing me forward gently. "And then let me take you home."

I do as he says, gathering some of my school books and a few clothes that aren't completely useless. And then I follow Silas out, my heart sinking slightly.

Cora Rose

I know that I joked about it before, but I really don't know what I'm going to do. I got this apartment on a whim, a last-minute Hail Mary. Murphy was a little stinky and Meena was loud, but the rent was cheap, and despite our landlord most likely stuffing dead bodies in the wall, it was a place to lay my head at night.

And now I have to figure out what to do. Because even though Silas said I could stay with him, I can't do it forever.

I need to get back on my own two feet alone.

"I can stay with you for a little while," I tell him when he pulls back up into his garage. He turns the car off and then faces me, his eyebrows drawn down.

"You can stay as long as you need."

"Thank you, Dr. Sinclair...Silas, but honestly this could get you into trouble, right?"

"What could get me into trouble is me licking your asshole in my office. You staying with me can just be...kept between us."

I manage a small, wobbly smile.

Why is he being so nice to me? I mean, yeah, he wants to fuck me, but that doesn't mean he needs to offer his spare room to me. He's going above and beyond, and I don't quite understand it.

"Are you sure? I can get a motel..."

"Forget it. Get your ass out of the car and we'll do a load of laundry. I can smell the dirty roof water on your clothes and it's not appealing."

He leads me inside, and I throw my clothes into the washer before sinking down onto the couch and setting my books out on the coffee table to dry.

"At least I had my laptop on me," I say, more to myself than anything.

"Yes, that's a good thing. That would be harder to replace. Everything else can be bought."

He sinks down next to me and our legs brush.

To be honest, right in this moment, besides wanting to laugh at the absurdity of it all, I also kind of want to cry into his shoulder. I want him to hold me close and let me fall asleep in his arms.

"What a fucking day," he murmurs as his fingers flex into a fist. It sits on his thigh and I want it to reach out and hold on to me, like he did back at my apartment.

But it doesn't move, just twitches on his leg.

I press the palm of my hand into my eye and let out a puff of air. "I mean, you did have a pretty hot date."

He turns to look at me. "And so did you. Although, they did seem more interested in each other."

I huff a laugh. "That they did. In fact, as we left, I think LoveJoy was sitting on Garrett's lap."

"Yeah, he probably tied him down with all those ribbons." A very unseemly snort escapes Silas's nose, and I can't help but grin.

Fuck, he's funny in a weird, unhinged way. I like it. I like it a lot.

"Yeah, I can see Garrett liking all that. He's really into shiny things."

Silas lets out another small laugh and then sighs. "Hell," he mutters as his hand unfurls from his thigh and slides across my shoulders.

He pulls me into him, and I bury my face in his chest, inhaling the scent of him. Sex and cum and something inherently Silas. He's so fucking hot.

"God, you must be exhausted. What a long fucking day," he murmurs into my hair.

I sigh and lay on him a little further. He's so warm and comforting, and honestly, I could use a long-drawn-out hug.

"Let's shower and get into bed," he tells me.

I should get up because a naked, wet Silas is the thing of dreams, but I honestly don't want to move from my place on top of him. I wiggle against him, bringing both our bodies down against the couch cushions and bury my face into his neck.

"Don't wanna move," I murmur.

His hands slide up my back and into my hair, holding me against him.

And even though my cock's been hard and his is growing against my leg, at this point in time, I have no desire to act on it. I just want to be with Silas, just let him comfort me.

It's really been a shit show, and I need someone to help me mop up the mess.

"You're very muscly and heavy," he grunts as I continue to lie on top of him.

I smile against his skin. "Yeah, but you love all my muscles."

"Hm," he replies. "Perhaps."

"You do, admit it."

He huffs again, and I reach under his armpit and tickle him, causing him to gasp and writhe beneath me.

"You better fucking not," he hisses, but it only makes me want to do it more.

I dig my fingers into his pit and he bucks beneath me, kind of like a rodeo rider. I could get on that. Would be nicer if I was sitting on his dick. Although, to be fair, it's right there, grinding up against me. Tickling him hasn't made it go down. In fact, it only seems to grow harder.

"Your dick likes this and you do too," I laugh as he tries to get me off of him. It doesn't work. I hold on like the pro I am.

A snort escapes him and then a giggle, and by the time I roll off him, he has tears streaming down his cheeks.

"I'm going to kill you," he wheezes, swiping at his eyes.

"As long as you murder me with your dick, we'll be just fine."

Full Service

He rolls his eyes and then sits up, trying to compose himself, but I wrecked him. He looks positively delicious.

My eyes are telling him what I'm thinking because he purses his lips and shakes his head. "Absolutely not. We are keeping this professional, starting now."

I glance down at my dick and sigh.

"Sorry, buddy," I tell it, and Silas chuckles lowly.

"Yes, sorry is right. If you're going to stay here, it needs to be."

"Right, totally professional," I say and then our eyes clash and I crawl toward him, sitting right between his legs. I gaze up at him and see his pupils dilate.

"How about we start that tomorrow instead? This will just be our little secret."

When he doesn't respond right away, I continue, "I mean, we already did shit today, might as well keep it going."

His brow furrows. He's thinking about it, really considering my proposition.

"I suppose you do make a very good point."

My tongue sneaks out and wets my lips. "Yeah, I mean, we already broke the rules. We can start again tomorrow." *Or the next day*, I think.

"Fine, but none of this on campus."

I mean, no promises, but if it gets me closer to his dick again, then fuck yes.

"What do you want to do?" I ask as I reach out and drag my hands up those thighs. They flex under my touch, and I feel a tremor move through him. Hell yes, he wants this. He's just as excited as me.

"I think it's time I show off how well my knees work."

* * *

I nearly pass out when Silas drops to his knees beside me, his hair still disheveled, his shirt unbuttoned. I want him completely naked. Well, that's not entirely true. I could do with a rumpled professor between my legs. I love it more than I should. Makes me think of that night he sat in that chair and came.

My dream come true.

"You can't be serious," I say, my voice raspy and shaking slightly. "God, you're trying to kill me, aren't you?"

"Perhaps. Perhaps it's your turn to beg."

My dick perks up at that and my eyes nearly cross when he reaches between us and brazenly grabs on to my cock. His fingers squeeze me roughly, and I arch my hips up, wanting more friction. I want more. Need it.

"On the couch, pants off."

I nearly trip, trying to do what he says, and when I'm finally bare from the waist down, Silas crawls closer to me, shuffling right between my legs and pulling my balls out with his hand. Just that touch has me groaning loudly. I'm going to bring the house down at this rate. The neighbors will call the cops and have me arrested. But what did Silas expect when he asked me to stay with him?

A horny man in his early twenties?

Jesus, this was just asking for trouble.

If he keeps with cutting this off tomorrow, my dick is going to fall off. I won't survive it.

"Sit on your hands," he tells me gruffly, and I blink down at him, unsure if I heard him right.

"Yeah, you heard me. Hands under that sexy ass of yours. And no coming until I say so."

"But your mouth is going to be busy."

"Oh, trust me. I'll manage."

I bet he will. He's a professional.

Full Service

I do as he says, pressing my hands under my thighs and watching as he drags his nose up my thigh and right to the crease of my groin. I let out a shaky breath as his tongue snakes across the base of me. My cock leaks profusely, precum coating my head as he licks his way to my tip. He laps me up, tasting my essence. I want to unload into his mouth, right down his throat.

I want to watch him gag on me, swallow me whole.

I bite my lip in anticipation of what's to come. But then something occurs to me and I glance over at the fish tank.

"Cover the fish tank first," I say, and Silas glances up at me, clearly confused. "I don't want her to jump out of her tank in protest."

He nods once, standing and tossing a blanket over it, effectively covering the entire thing.

"Privacy, at last," he says with a grin and then slides between my legs once more. "Are you ready, Mr. Winslow?"

The way he says my name makes my dick jump.

"Fuck yes."

And he doesn't disappoint. Seconds later, his eyes lock on to mine as he sucks the head of my cock between his lips. They stretch around my tip, and I arch up into him, wanting him to take more of me.

But he doesn't give me what I want. Instead, he teases me with his tongue, sliding it through my slit, making me moan and grunt, nearly begging for more.

It's when I finally cave and whisper *"please"* that he takes more of me into him, an inch, just a fucking inch. So I just chant that word over and over, pleading with him.

He finally takes pity on me and swallows me whole, his nose pressed into my neatly trimmed pubic hairs. He holds me there, his throat constricting around my hard length, making my eyes cross, making my breath come out in pained whimpers.

My fingers curl under my legs, and I try like hell to keep

them off his head. He wants to control this, which is hot as fuck, and I can tell he's getting off on edging me. He brings me right to the brink over and over until I'm a sweating, sobbing mess.

"Silas," I moan, my eyes screwed shut, my abdomen flexing tightly, trying to stave off my orgasm. The flat of his tongue slides along my cockhead as he sucks on my tip like a lollipop.

"Hm?" he hums, and I blink my eyes open. The room swims, the only thing constant is him, kneeling before me. His lips pink and puffy, his cheeks flushed red.

"Are you trying to give me a heart attack?" I rasp.

His eyes sparkle and he sits up, leaving my spit-covered dick to nearly weep.

"No," he says as he grabs me behind my knees and tugs me forward, my ass nearly off the couch now. I'm slouched down, my hands slipping behind my back.

"Better," he says, wetting his lips and then pushing my knees up against my chest, exposing me fully.

Fuck yes, I think as he pushes my balls up and swipes the tip of his tongue across my hole. He moans as he does it, telling me how much he enjoys eating ass. It's a rare find, not many people would want to do this.

Not many people have done this to me, which makes Silas a fucking gem.

He slides his tongue around my rim, pushing in gently and making me arch my hips up, wanting to give him better access. He's really fucking good at this, his mouth making me sloppy and wet.

"More. Please," I moan, but of course he makes me wait, rimming me gently until I'm panting and whining. It's only when I'm nearly crying in frustration that he pushes his tongue all the way inside of me.

I cry out, my body shaking with need. And he continues his assault, making me a writhing, moaning mess, my cock leaking profusely, precum dripping down the sides, needing to come and yet unable to touch myself to do so.

If only I could come untouched like Silas.

Fuck, has he come already?

If he has, that is so hot.

His tongue suddenly leaves me, my hole open and gaping, and then his finger slides inside of me, crooking and finding my prostate. I cry out again, my heart thumping wildly in my chest.

"Not yet, Mr. Winslow," he grumbles as he takes my cock back into his mouth, sucking up all the precum with one swallow and making me bow up off the couch.

I'm chanting nonsense now, just jumbled words as he continues to work my prostate with his fingers and my cock with his mouth.

He really is good on his knees.

When he slides two fingers inside of me, my hole constricts, and I let out a pained moan. Not from being stretched open, but from being unable to find my release.

But Silas doesn't give in, he just continues the assault until I'm nearly blacking out from the pleasure of it.

"You can come now," he finally says, and I blink my eyes open as he swallows me down once more, his hand bobbing furiously on the base of my cock, his fingers working in and out of me, brushing blissfully against my pleasure spot.

I come with a shout, my vision whiting out as ropes of cum shoot into his mouth and down his throat. And he doesn't stop sucking until I'm wrung dry. It's only then that he pulls his fingers from me and his mouth off my dick. He crawls up on the couch, straddles me, pulls his own cock out, and slides it between my open lips.

I take him, eagerly, letting him use my mouth as a fuck toy until he too is spilling his seed onto my tongue.

When it's over, he slouches over me, his body shaking, his

cock softening in my mouth. I keep him inside of me as long as he lets me, and when he finally slips from my opening, he falls to my side and presses a hand to his eyes.

He's wrecked, disheveled. The same as me.

"Dr. Sinclair," I rasp and lean over, pressing my body against his. I'm half-clothed and his pants are around his thighs, but neither of us makes a move to fix ourselves up. We just hold on to each other while we come down from the high of it.

"Mr. Winslow," he replies after a deep inhale. "We have a few more hours."

I nod as I kiss my way up his neck and nibble on his ear.

"I just need like two minutes to get hard again."

He chuckles. "I need longer than that. I'm old."

"You are not. At least your knees aren't. They held up really well."

"I was motivated," he says with a laugh.

I burrow in further, realizing that my weight may be suffocating, but he doesn't stop me, just holds me a little tighter.

Minutes later he shifts beneath me, and I feel the whisper of his voice against my skin. "As well as my knees held up, my back might not. Want to move this to the bedroom?"

Fuck yes, I do. I nearly launch upright, pulling up my pants and striding toward his bedroom.

"We have two hours until midnight," I tell him and then throw myself on the bed and kick my pants off. "We can get at least two more orgasms in by then."

Silas follows me down.

"I think you're a little confused," he says as his lips meet mine. "I'm thinking at least ten."

Chapter Twelve

Everly

I can't move. Silas sucked my dick so many times and fucked my mouth incessantly last night, and now my entire body aches.

God, what will full-on sex be like with him?

I probably won't survive. Whoever finds me will find an empty, dried husk of a man. I'll be left for the crows.

The smell of breakfast wakes me up, and I stretch out on his bed.

I slept here last night, passed out in our mess. *God, he probably hated that,* I think with a huff as I roll over, the sheets sticking to me. So much cum.

Buckets galore.

I stare down at my chest and run a hand over it, grinning to myself. I wanna do that again.

Silas was true to his word, we didn't fuck past midnight. But that was fine by me. By the time the clock struck twelve, I was so worn out, I thought I was going to die.

He's sucked and fucked my soul right out of me.

I'm hoping this morning he forgets about this silly rule he has about keeping things professional because now that I've had a taste, I really don't want to go back to the way things were.

I stand up and walk into the bathroom, taking a quick shower and pulling on a pair of his boxer shorts. He's not as bulky as me, so they're a little tight. Perfection. Now he can see the bulge I'm sporting for him.

I stride out to the kitchen, finding Silas at the stove, wearing a t-shirt and joggers.

God, this man is delicious. The way he fills out these casual clothes.

So damn tempting.

"Morning," I say, my voice low and hoarse. Probably from my throat being fucked.

Silas turns his dark gaze over at me and his eyes move slowly over my half-nude form.

"You're wearing my boxers."

"Sure am," I say as I take a seat at the small island, watching his ass as he moves.

Wanna fuck that too.

"It's almost ready," he tells me, his voice cracking slightly. Seems he's just as wrecked as me. I love that when he goes to give a lecture, every word that spills from his mouth will remind him of me.

Makes me hard just thinking of it.

"Coffee is right over there, if you want some," he says, pointing to a French press sitting on the stove. *Of course he has one of these*, I think as I stand and grab a mug. I make sure to brush against him as much as possible as I move about, wanting to respect his wishes, but also reminding him of what he's missing.

"Creamer?" I ask, and he nods, pointing to the fridge.

I pull it out—organic. Must be nice.

Full Service

"Think I'll like living here," I murmur as I pour a hefty amount into my mug.

"Well," he begins, clearing his throat. "It should be fine as we both have very busy schedules."

"Right," I say, taking another seat and sipping on the hot brew. Silas sets a plate down in front of me, an egg and sausage scramble.

Sure would like to scramble his eggs with my sausage.

I dig in, burning my mouth slightly as I go, but hell, this is real nice. I like this a lot.

"Thanks," I say around a mouthful. Silas eyes me with an arched eyebrow and nods.

"Of course. I won't be making your breakfast every morning though. You'll have to fend for yourself."

"You just wanted to thank me for last night," I tease. "I see how it is."

He huffs and then takes a sip of his coffee, picking at his food.

"Well, we can call it a one-off. Like I said, it won't happen again."

I groan, but keep eating. I mean, I really want it to happen again. And again. I won't pressure him, but I can entice him.

Really let him know what he's missing out on.

"Are you going to work today?" I ask, and he nods.

"Have some committee meetings to attend."

"Snooze," I snort, and he grins.

"Yeah, basically. But it's part of my contract so...."

We grin at one another and then I focus on shoving the food into my mouth, burping lightly when I'm done. I set the plate in the sink and then decide to wash it. It's only polite.

When I'm done, I spin around and catch Silas's eyes on my ass. My teeth bite my lip to keep a smile at bay. This fucker. He knows what he wants.

And he wants me.

"Alright, well, I'm going to get changed and head to campus for a bit, then maybe meet with my dad. Can you drive me to get my car?" I ask, and he straightens up and nods. He opens a drawer and pulls out a house key, holding it up to me.

"For you," he says, and my heart flutters in my chest. Feels like he's my boyfriend or some shit, which is ridiculous. I've never wanted a boyfriend.

Until now.

Fuck.

This is just my luck. I want a man who has set up strict boundaries.

No more touching. Professionalism all the way.

I can so do that. I can be the most professional.

* * *

After class and a short shift at the club, I make my way to my dad's place. Parking in the lot and groceries in bags around my wrist, I traverse the densely packed trailer park. I can see my dad's truck and camper in the distance and pick up my pace. He's been working a construction job here for the past few months before he heads off to the next place. It's been nice having him here, and with his busy schedule, I realize that he's probably not been making himself actual food.

Been living off frozen dinners and beer, I'm sure. That can't be healthy.

My mind flashes to Dr. Sinclair, and I bite back a smile. I wonder if he goes home and cooks himself dinner or if he has a freezer full of frozen dinners too.

Hm, I'll have to see about that.

Maybe I'll have to start cooking him dinners too.

Now that's an idea.

Full Service

"Ev!" my dad says, exiting his trailer, a beer in his hand. He looks so much like me, wide shoulders and blond hair, but twenty-four years older, and a little more rugged.

He's always joked that I'm the reason he has wrinkles near his eyes. Apparently, I was a wild child. I got in trouble more than I should have growing up, but then again, it was never anything serious. Just stupid kid stuff. And my dad was too busy to really get angry over it. He usually just shook his head and pinched his nose in frustration.

"Hey," I say, holding up my arms, the plastic bags dangling there. "I'm making you dinner."

"Nothing healthy, I hope."

"Just a side salad. But we're doing steak and potatoes."

His lips quirk up. "Deal. Let me get the grill out."

He disappears around the back of the trailer and reappears a moment later with a portable grill, setting it up and attaching a propane tank to the underneath.

I set my stuff down in a chair and walk inside, washing my hands and taking a look around. This was a trailer my dad bought after I graduated high school when he started to work in different places along the West Coast. It was a cheap, old trailer with questionable choices in upholstery, but my dad, Joe, is a simple man and doesn't seem to mind it.

I pull the fridge open and grab a beer, twisting the cap off and taking a swig.

My face bunches up as I swallow it down. Never really did like beer, but then again, it's always what I drank with my dad. Probably when I shouldn't have. But it's kind of our thing.

"Got some new seasoning to try with the steak," I say, and my dad bunches his nose.

"A.1. Sauce is just fine. Don't need no spices."

"Dad. If you're using A.1. Sauce on steak, it's not good."

"Works just fine for me," he says and then grins.

My eyes roll as I get to work, turning the grill on and prepping my space. I know what he's doing. He's egging me on, trying to get under my skin. He's always done this. It's a subtle art with him, and I try to not let him win.

But I know when he does. His lips quirk up and his eyes twinkle.

Fucking dads, man.

"So, what's new with you? Haven't seen you in ages."

My eyes roll again as I set the steaks on the grill and place a pot on the burner.

"Pour the potatoes in the pot, old man. And I was here last week."

"Hm, seems my old mind has forgotten already."

"You're forty-five. You're not old."

"Feel like it," he says gruffly. "Had a kid who was kind of a brat. Took years off my life."

I scoff at that and then nudge him. "Quit it. Or I'll make you eat *two* bowls of salad."

"Not two bowls," he grumbles as he takes another swig of beer and then haphazardly stirs the instant mashed potatoes.

I was gonna go for the real thing, but it would take too much prep work. And to be honest, my dad prefers the instant potatoes anyways. He's bougie like that.

"Two bowls," I repeat and then we grin stupidly at one another. "So, how long are you here for? Where are you off to next?"

"Up to Redding after this. Probably stay there through the summer."

"Gonna be a hot one."

"Yep," he says and nods. "But after that, I'll try to take something closer to you in the fall. Hopefully."

My heart warms at that. For as unique as my childhood was, growing up with him as my father, he really did the best he could. And he's always put me first. Hasn't even dated, probably never even considered it. His focus was on providing for me.

"May even have a bonus check that I can give you—"

"Hell no. You keep your money. I don't want it."

He sighs. "A dad should be able to pay for his kid's school, son."

"Yeah, but I've got this. I have a good job." I don't mention the caved-in ceiling or the fact that I am technically homeless. I know that he'd feel the need to do something, and I can't have that. He needs to take care of himself. He gave up so much for me growing up, caring for me as a single dad. I need him to not worry about me, to just take this time for himself.

He arches his eyebrow at me. "One where you have to strip?"

"Yeah, but I'm good at it."

"If your grandfather knew what you did."

I roll my eyes. "He'd probably cheer me on. He's just as deviant as me."

My dad grins widely and shakes his head. "Probably right. He tried to rope me into some kind of sensual ribbon dance at the old folks' home."

"What the hell is that?" I ask with a laugh.

"No clue, but I told him no fucking way. I'm sure he'll ask you next."

"I would give a good show. Just don't know if I have the time to commit."

My dad hums his agreement. "Anything to get out of that shit show."

"I mean, yeah. I guess I'll tell him I'm too busy, but we do need to show up and support him."

"I don't know what sensual ribbon dancing means, and I honestly don't know if I want to see my dad shimmying up on stage."

I let out a laugh as I dish up the steaks on plates and scoop out some mashed potatoes. My dad looks glumly at the salad I hand him, but he eats it first, almost shoveling it into his mouth to get it out of the way.

When we're done with dinner, we sit outside his camper, drinking beer and just shooting the shit. I tell him about my classes and about my job as a TA. I don't mention Dr. Sinclair at all, not wanting him to read the expression on my face if I do. He'd read me like a fucking book.

I can already tell he doesn't like the idea of me stripping. I don't want to tell him I'm acting inappropriately with the professor I'm supposed to be working for.

And that last night, he got down on his knees and sucked my dick. And I did the same.

No, no that won't do.

So instead, I keep this entire thing to myself. Out of respect for Dr. Sinclair and for my sanity. I don't need to be getting all up in my head about this. There's a very good chance this will all end terribly.

Doesn't stop me from trying though.

Even if I only get scraps from him, I want it.

After saying goodbye to my dad, I do what any college guy would do on a Friday night and head to Shenanigans, the local bar. My infatuation with Dr. Sinclair is nothing a drink or two can't solve. As I push my way to the bar top, I see Perry, the bartender, flirting with a guy with a head full of curls. Curly-hair-guy flirts right back, and who could blame him? Perry is hot. All that tanned skin and those whiskey-colored eyes. They're almost hypnotic. If I wasn't obsessing over Silas, then maybe I'd be interested.

Seems I only have eyes for a forbidden man.

"Hey there," Perry says when he catches my gaze. "What are you having tonight?"

I cock an eyebrow at him and tap my fingers against my lips. "How about a whiskey sour."

"Hm, I like it. Matches my eyes, you flirt."

"Oh my god. Stop it," the other guy says.

"Aw, come on, Puppy. I'm cute when I flirt," Perry tells him.

"You're always cute."

"Not as cute as you," Perry winks at him, then looks in my direction. "He's my boyfriend. Isn't he hot?"

I eye the guy. Yeah, I mean, he is, but it seems like if I say that I'll get in trouble. "Can we get back to my drink now?"

"Oh yeah, the drink that's like your eyes..." Puppy says. I don't know what the guy's actual name is. Clearly, I can tell they're just being playful, and these two only have eyes for each other.

"I wasn't flirting with you, just so you know," I clarify.

He grabs some bottles and starts making my drink.

"Um, are you sure you aren't flirting with me? When Puppy and I first met, he was flirting with me without even knowing."

Puppy shakes his head, his curly hair flopping onto his forehead. "No, I wasn't. I just didn't know you were flirting with me."

I let out a loud laugh and then lean forward, making sure they can hear me.

"No worries, really. I have a thing going with someone right now."

"Oh, really? This is getting good," the boyfriend says.

"Yep. Someone forbidden."

Perry's eyes twinkle, dancing in the lights of the bar. "Tell us more. We do love a good forbidden romance."

"It's not romance. It's obsession."

"Well, I certainly didn't expect to hear that. Sounds fun though. Care to share who this obsession is with?"

I shake my head as I take a sip of my drink. Just like with my dad, I keep that little tidbit tucked away inside of me. I don't want Dr. Sinclair to get into trouble because of me. I want him to lust after me, not hate me.

"Well, fine. Don't share with us. But if you ever need someone to talk to, let us know. We're awesome at relationship stuff." Perry winks at his man.

I don't remind him my thing is more about obsession and pocket that friendly suggestion, taking another large gulp. The bourbon hits me hard, and I cough slightly.

"I'll keep you both in mind. Thanks."

I reach over to pay, and he accepts it, charging me with a flick of his wrist. A moment later, Perry wanders off to help someone else. My gaze lifts to the mirror behind the bar top, and I see myself reflected back. My eyes are alight, my skin flushed, my stomach fluttering in anticipation of going home and seeing Silas again.

Yeah, seems I'm fooling myself. Seems that this forbidden thing may be a little more than obsession.

Chapter Thirteen

Silas

I will behave like the mature man I am when I get home. I will not stare at Everly's ass when he walks in the door, and I will not touch my dick when he bends over.

I will not.

I refuse.

But it seems my eyeballs and hands are staging a revolt because they're wandering to places they should not be going. It doesn't help that Everly's jeans are hanging down low and he's not wearing underwear. His ass crack is showing, all sleek and smooth. I want to run my tongue up it.

"How was your day?" Everly asks, bending down to shuffle through his bag. He's doing this on purpose. He's giving me a long-drawn-out view of his ass. He knows exactly what's going on with me right now.

I glance down at my cock and sigh, placing a throw pillow over my lap.

I will not lust.

"Fine," I say and then ask, "Yours?"

"Meh, same. Saw my dad," he tells me as he stands up and walks toward me. My dick pushes into the pillow with extreme force, wanting to burst through the stuffing.

"How was it?"

"Good," he says, lowering himself down far too close to me. There is a whole couch and he sits right next to me. Honestly.

He leans back and spreads his arms out, placing one behind me. But that's not what I'm focused on. I'm focused on his crotch. His dick.

It's half hard.

At this rate, there's a nine percent chance I will remain professional and mature.

"There is an entire couch, you know," I grumble, and Everly turns toward me, his dirty-blond hair flopping onto his forehead. I have to dig my fingers into the pillow to keep from reaching out.

"Yeah, but I like it fine right here."

I huff and then try to scoot over, but really can't manage more than an inch. And when I do, he just spreads his legs wider and knocks into mine.

I'm set ablaze.

"Man," he says, pulling up his shirt and scratching at his chest. It's unfair really. He's putting me in the most dire of situations. I start to sweat, my face and dick leaking. This is preposterous.

I am an adult. I have restraint.

"Do you mind if I jack off?" he asks, and my eyes nearly bug out of my head.

"What?" I ask, since I'm positive I'm hallucinating.

"I've had a long day and want to get off. Is that cool?"

Of course it's not cool. It's ridiculous. I will not have him pulling his dick out and masturbating in my living room.

"Fine. It's fine."

He grins and then reaches down, pulling his thick, veiny dick out, and starts to stroke it. I will not stare at it like a man in heat. I am mature.

"You can do it too, you know. Just two bros, jerking it after a long day."

I scoff and press the pillow into my lap harder.

I'm not going to jerk off while he's jerking off. That's not what bros do.

Everly leans his head back and groans, his dick spurting a little precum. I tasted that. Had my mouth around it and drank from it like a fountain. This is obscene. This is indecent.

"Oh god, that feels good," he says. "Just what I needed."

I eye it and see that it probably does feel good. Much better than what I'm doing. Which is nothing.

"You should try it. Really will take the tension out of your neck and back," Everly says, and I pull my lips between my teeth. That comment is silly. It does not do any such thing.

A low groan escapes him, and I reach between the pillow and my lap and give my dick a good squeeze.

I can see Everly watching me, his pupils blown out, his cheeks flushed red.

"Take it out," he says, and I let out a gasp at the wanton demand. "Take it out and jerk it."

"I am not a bro," I grumble, but I'm already taking my cock out, throwing the pillow to the side and stroking it. Oh god. Yes. That feels divine. Like heaven. Like pie. Apple pie.

"Awesome," Everly breathes, eyeing my dick. "Feels good huh?"

"Yes," is all I can muster. I'm about to blow just from the scent of him. This is unheard of.

"Wish you could suck my dick again. Lick my hole. Felt really good," he says on a moan and then arches his hips up, fucking into his fist. "But I know we're gonna be professional, so I'll just relive it in my brain instead."

Sounds like a grand idea, and very reasonable.

We stroke our cocks, skin on skin until we're both breathing heavily, our chests heaving.

He leans toward me, our faces turned toward one another, and our lips brush, just a taste, a fluke. And then with a grunt, Everly comes, shooting cum across his chest. The sight and smell push me over the edge. I join him, releasing into my hand with his name on my lips.

"Hell yes," Everly says and then closes his eyes, pulling his shirt off and wiping himself up. He doesn't even wash his hands. I should not take the shirt he's offering me and clean myself up, but I do. I wipe up the mess I made all over my hands and groin and then continue to sit there, trying like hell to keep my composure. But it's hard when he's leaning into me, his head landing on my shoulder.

This is a terrible idea.

And yet, I do nothing to stop it.

* * *

I'm mostly not surviving this. It's incredible how hot Everly is and how he flaunts it without even trying. I'm currently sitting at dinner with Lee, trying to not get a boner while he prattles on about the ribbon dance which is happening next weekend.

God help me. I don't want to fling a ribbon around any more than I want to stop jerking off with Everly.

I shift in my seat, trying like hell to keep my focus, but finding it very hard. Everything reminds me of Everly. That peach painting that's hanging on the wall to my left, it reminds me of his butt.

And the cucumber that woman is eating on the patio is reminiscent of his dick.

And good God, even the beige wallpaper is making me think of his flawless skin, more golden than anything, smooth and rippled with muscles.

I shift in my seat, my dick hard now.

"Why are you squirming in your seat? Does your butt itch?" Lee asks, and I frown at him.

"My butt does not itch."

"Are you sure? Do you wash it good? Sometimes men forget to do that. I've been known to."

"Lee, absolutely not. I am not talking to you about butt holes while you eat meatloaf."

He grins at me and takes an obscenely big bite of it. "I thought you were a fan of meat."

I let out a horrified laugh and then toss a napkin at him.

"Wipe your face, old man. You have ketchup on your chin."

He doesn't wipe it up, just lets it sit.

God, this man is going to be the death of me.

Him and Everly.

"So, how's your love life?" he asks me. "LoveJoy showed up the other day with another man on his arm. When I asked him what happened to you, he said you ditched him on your date."

"I did not ditch him. I wandered off. He was too busy with jock-man to even pay any attention to me."

Lee grins at me, the glob of ketchup jiggling on his chin. "Ah, who did you wander off with?"

"Someone." When he arches an eyebrow at me, I roll my eyes. "Someone that's none of your business."

His eyes twinkle. "Well, let me know if you want to meet my grandson. He's quite the catch."

"I think I've had enough of the dating scene," I say, and Lee takes another large mouthful. The ketchup slips a little further down his chin.

"Let me know when you change your mind."

I won't. I already have enough temptation to last me until my dying day. It's one of the reasons I'm out with Lee at his favorite diner and not back at home. Because I know that if I go back, I'm going to sit on that sofa and jack my dick. Right next to Everly's. Our lips brushing, me fighting and losing the battle to remain professional.

I really need to stop.

It's been a week and I haven't been able to say no to him. Every evening, I tell my body to go to my room, but I end up sitting on the couch, pretending to watch TV until he gets home.

Then when he arrives, he lowers himself down next to me, smelling like soap after a shower, or like sweat after a long day out, and he pulls that fat cock out and fucks it with his fist.

And I can't help but join in.

I really don't want him feeling left out.

I'd hate for him to feel uncomfortable in my space. I told him to make himself at home.

He has.

"I won't change my mind. I'm going to stay single."

"You make a sad single man, Silas. You're lonely."

I am, and I didn't quite realize how much until Everly moved in with me. It's been nice having him around, even if our schedules are a little out of sync. But it's nice to come home to him. I look forward to it.

Last night he even made me dinner.

It melted my cold, dark heart a little.

"Yeah, and what about you? Any love prospects?"

He shrugs, that deviant glint in his eyes. "Do you really want to know?"

Full Service

I stare at that ketchup and shake my head. I really don't. I'm sure it's something that will make my stomach turn.

"Actually, I'd rather not, Lee."

He chuckles and then proceeds to talk about ribbon dance choreography, and I just sit there nodding, my dick once more perking up at the thought of Everly.

By the time I get back home, he's on the couch, his hand down his pants, his eyes on the door. Almost like he was waiting for me to come home.

Oh, who am I kidding? He was so waiting for me to come home.

"Hey," he says, his voice lower than normal. "You're late."

"I was meeting with a friend."

His hand stops moving, and he sits up slightly. "A platonic friend?"

"Yes," I say as I strip my coat off and move toward him. He relaxes and spreads his legs out.

I take a seat right next to him, our thighs pressed together as I work my pants open. My dick is already hard and ready. Everly holds the lube out for me, and I let him squirt some in my palm. It's a really nice brand, the kind that glides down dicks really smoothly.

I can feel his gaze on me, and I work my hand faster, basking in the feel of his admiration. He likes what he sees. I know he does. He always thanks me afterward.

I feel like a motherfucking king.

My eyes fall to his cock, and I watch as it leaks, precum beading on the tip before he swipes it away with his thumb. I want to engulf it with my mouth, but I don't. Of course not. This is professional.

The utmost.

"Oh fuck," he grunts as he arches his hips up. I can imagine so many things in this moment. I can imagine that I'm fucking into him and he's driven wild by the slide of my dick in his hole. Or that he's pushing that cock into me and losing all control from being strangled by my tight, willing ass.

Somehow I end up moving. I'm suddenly on top of him, pushing him back and straddling his legs.

His eyes darken, his lips parting in a groan.

"Fuck yes."

Our dicks touch as we stroke them, working ourselves to release.

"I thought you wanted to keep it professional?" he says, and I nod, trying like to hell to be reasonable.

"I will. I will. This is so professional," I pant, and he nods.

"It is. I think kissing is professional too," he whimpers, and I agree. I missed him all goddamn day. I've been waiting for this. What's a little kiss? What does it matter what we do at home?

It doesn't, a little voice whispers in the back of my mind, and I let go, pushing my mouth to his. He groans as my tongue sweeps into him, tangling with his tongue, tasting him.

"I'm coming," he sighs, pulling away from me slightly and then lets out a sweet groan, "*Silas.*"

It's my name on his lips that has my hand working faster and as soon as he explodes, I topple over the edge as well, ruining my shirt in the process. I really need to remove it before sitting down. Perhaps, we should just sit naked from now on. Less laundry, and really, it's saving the environment.

"Fuck, that's a lot of cum," Everly says, looking at my limp dick resting against his.

"Yeah. Was saving it up all damn day," I say, causing him to snort.

"Yeah. Me too."

He winks at me, and my cheeks flush. He leans forward and kisses me softly, making me whimper against his lips.

"Fuck, you taste so good," he says gently, and I nod.

Full Service

"You do too."

We stare at each other, deeply. Our eyes never leaving the other's, but then I hear the neighbor's car start loudly, and it breaks us out of our stupor.

"So, um," Everly says clearing his throat. "What's the plan? Did you already have dinner?" he asks.

I reach over for some tissues, an industrial-sized box I picked up last week. I hand him one and he starts to wipe himself up.

"I already ate."

"Bummer. Is it okay if I have one of your frozen dinners?" he asks, looking almost shy.

"You can have anything you'd like," I tell him and then stand up, pulling my shirt off, making Everly's eyes fall to my chest.

"Anything?" he asks suggestively.

My hand flexes near my side. Good God, he makes it hard.

Makes me hard.

"Anything," I say and then tilt my head toward the hallway. "I'm going to go shower."

He nods and stands up, his dick still out of his jeans, looking delicious. I need to shower stat. Before I do something ridiculous.

Like fall to my knees.

I've been doing so well. I've been so professional.

I've been like seven percent professional.

"See you tomorrow?" I ask, and he nods.

"Tomorrow."

And as I walk away, I can feel his eyes on me, and tomorrow feels like eons away.

* * *

I don't know when I changed my mind about being professional, but sometime in the middle of the following week, I snap. Maybe it's the fact that the nightly jerk-off sessions with Everly have worn me down. Or maybe it's because I hear him every morning getting off in the shower.

He makes no effort to be quiet about it. He moans my name like it's a sin.

I stand outside the door and get off too.

Like the pervert I've become.

But I think what really pushed me over the edge was Wednesday, my birthday. I've told no one about it, but still, I pout the entire day because I've received no calls. Not even a text message. Even my sister forgot about it. Not that I expect her to remember. She has her own life, and we were never big on birthdays growing up. She's not to blame.

Lee doesn't mention it either, but then again, how could he? He doesn't know.

I just like to feel sorry for myself, it seems.

I'm thirty-six now, one more year closer to death.

When I arrive back to my place that night, I plan to sulk about and drink a gallon of wine and wait for Everly to return. Maybe I'll tell him, and he can help me celebrate. Maybe he'll let me smear him with cake and lick it off him.

What's the point of professionalism when I'm going to die anyways?

What's the point of living if I never live?

I'm contemplating my entire life. Growing older does this to a person. It makes you wonder what the hell you've been doing all your life. I got my doctorate at a young age, got a great job, and yet here I am…single. My best friend is a ninety-two-year-old dude. And I have no love life.

I'm unhappy.

Fuck, I just want to be happy.

"I can be happy," I grumble to myself as I enter my place. I drop the keys into the small ceramic bowl, and when I flick my gaze up, I see Everly. He's naked, wearing only a jock strap, and standing in the middle of the living room, a chocolate cupcake in his hand.

A fucking present if I ever saw one.

I just stare at him, my eyes watering slightly at the sentiment.

How did he know? How the fuck did he know?

He must register the shock on my face because he smiles and says, "I went through your mail. It told me it was your birthday," he explains and then shrugs, his nipples puckering the closer I get.

"You didn't have to do this," I say as he pulls out a lighter and lights the single pink candle.

"I did."

He starts to sing "Happy Birthday" and fuck me, he has a nice voice. It's low, husky. Makes my dick perk up.

Oh, who am I kidding? It was hard earlier. All day really. Just thinking of him.

When he's done, the song trailing off, he grins at me. "Make a wish, Silas."

He holds the chocolate cupcake out to me, and I pause, letting everything filter through my mind.

I wish that I wasn't lonely anymore.

I wish that I could fuck Everly.

I wish I could hold him as we sleep.

That's too many wishes, I think as I blow the candle out. Only one needs to come true. But as I watch the smoke slither up between us, our eyes lock.

I can have whatever I want. I don't need a wish to make it come true.

I can make it come true.

Motherfucking me.

The realization settles within me as Everly leads me over to a kitchen chair, lowering me into it.

"I'm going to feed this to you," he says softly as he crouches down before me. I watch as his skin shimmers golden in the dim light, watch as his fingers break part of the cupcake off and he holds it up to my mouth.

"I know that this isn't professional—"

"Fuck professional," I interrupt as I lean forward and pull that piece of cake between my lips. My tongue snakes around his fingers, and I watch as his blue eyes are eclipsed by black.

His breathing grows stuttered.

"Yeah. Fuck yeah. Fuck professional," he whispers back as he breaks off more cake and feeds it to me. I eat it all, letting him smear it across my lips, watching as his gaze darkens with each lick and bite. When I'm done, he leans forward, our breath intermingling as he kisses me clean, licking and lapping at my lips, sucking the bottom one into his mouth and making me groan.

When he pulls away, his lips red, he meets my gaze once more.

"Are you sure about his?" he asks, and I nod.

I want this too much. I want to make my own wishes come true.

I want to stop fighting it so hard.

For once in my life, I want to let myself be happy.

"Yeah."

He stands up and leans down once more, his face near mine, his lips sliding to the shell of my ear. "Then I'm going to give you a little birthday present."

I let out a shaky breath and watch as he fiddles with his phone. Music starts to blare from the speakers, slow and sensual, and I watch as he starts to roll his hips.

"Oh god," I moan as I reach down and grab on to my dick as he starts to give me a lap dance.

"You can touch. There are no rules here. This is for you. Just for you."

I reach out and without even questioning it, let my hands skate across his skin. His shoulders, his pecs, and down to his abdomen. Oh fuck. He feels so good, warm, strong.

Mine.

As the music plays through his phone, I continue touching, my fingers raking across him as he continues to grind against me, making me slowly lose my mind.

The heel of his palm drags down my dick, and I arch up into his touch.

"That's right. You're hard for me, aren't you, Dr. Sinclair?"

I groan as I bring him back down for another kiss. We move like this for a minute until he pulls away and glances down at my dick.

"Take it out, show me what I do to you," he says as he turns around and starts to cant his hips back and forth against my lap.

I do as he says, pulling my cock and balls out, my pants halfway down my thighs. He wets his lips, and I feel a spurt of precum slide from my slit just from the sight of it.

"Yes. So hot. You're so hot."

"So are you."

His eyes twinkle and he bites his bottom lip.

"Wanna see something?"

"Yes."

He widens his legs and bends over fully, giving me a glimpse of his ass so close to my face. It's then that I notice his wet crack, lube trickling out of him. Oh fuck.

Fuck.

He's wet for me. Prepped.

Without thinking, I drag my fingers up him, swirling my

fingertip around his hole before pushing it inside. It squelches as I enter him, showing me just how much he put inside himself. For this moment.

For me.

"Were you going to fuck me, Mr. Winslow?" I ask, my voice low, feeling the slutty professor make an appearance.

He lets out a shaky exhale.

"I was hoping you'd let me," he groans as I continue to fuck my finger in and out of him. I turn my wrist and crook my finger making him whimper.

"What about being professional?" I tease, and he moans as he starts to fuck himself back on my hand.

"You've been driving me crazy. Living with you. It's too much. I couldn't take it anymore. This was my Hail Mary, Silas."

I push a second finger into him and watch as he grinds against it. He wants it. He wants it so bad.

"It's Dr. Sinclair," I say darkly.

"Oh fuck. Oh fuck. Yes. I'm sorry. I..." he's trembling as I press against his prostate, making him cry out.

"It's fine. Mr. Winslow," I let his name hang between us as he continues to fuck back against my hand. The sight of it, the feel of his tight hole strangling my fingers only makes me hornier.

"Turn around," I say gruffly. "And give me my birthday present."

My fingers slip from him, and he does as I ask, straddling my hips. I slot my bare cock at his hole and he lets out a long exhale, sinking down on it. Doesn't even hesitate, just falls onto it.

The sensation of finally being inside of him makes me groan. Deep and feral as he takes me all the way inside, impaling himself on me.

Full Service

Then he just sits there, his fingers clutching my shoulders, his forehead meeting mine.

"You feel so good inside of me," he whispers.

"You feel good too. So fucking perfect."

My hands move down to grab on to his ass, and I arch my hips up a little, making him gasp.

"Oh shit. Oh fuck."

"Language," I say, and he shakes his head, swallowing.

"Please. Please. Fuck me, Dr. Sinclair," he begs and then kisses me, a rough, wild kiss that forces my hips up once more. My fingers dig into his ass as he rides me, the two of us working in tandem as we move. I hear the slap of his body against mine, his ass hitting my thighs as his hands slide into my hair, digging into my scalp.

We're reduced to grunting, whining messes, eating each other's faces as we fuck. He rides my dick so good.

Hands down, this is the best sex I've ever had.

I knew it would be. That's probably why I resisted him for so long. I knew that as soon as I was inside of him, or he was inside of me, I'd be ruined.

For anyone else.

I only want him.

"Touch me. Touch me. I'm not going to last," Everly groans, and I reach between us, fisting his cock. He's grunting and moaning, his body starting to shake, his orgasm starting to crest. And I'm not much better. It's a miracle that I've lasted this long. Some divine intervention wanted to grant me a birthday wish.

One I didn't even think to wish for.

"Oh fuck! *Fuck*," he cries out, and I feel his cock pulse in my hand. His cum jets out and coats my shirt. His hole clenches around my dick, and I can't resist. I empty inside of him, my thrusts growing frantic until we're finally done.

Satiated.

For the time being, at least.

"Happy fucking birthday, Silas," he says as he kisses me sweetly.

We don't break apart for a while, my dick still inside of him as we lazily make out. This is the best birthday present. This, right here. I could die a happy man tonight.

We make out for so long, neither of us rushing to part from the other, that I grow hard once more. As I fill out in his ass, he trembles against me, whispering that he can take it again. That he's not too sore.

That he's been waiting for this all his life.

So I give it to him again.

And again.

Happy birthday to me.

Chapter Fourteen

Silas

I think I like being unprofessional.

I feel lighthearted and happy.

I should have given in ages ago.

"Good morning, sleepy head," Everly says, his lips brushing against my neck.

I pull him up against me and drag my hands down to his ass. I squeeze those globes roughly.

He took me so good.

So fucking good. Each time.

"How did you sleep?" he asks as he threads his hands through my hair.

"Good."

"Because I slept with you?"

When I don't answer, he chuckles. "I know it's because I fucked your brains out and then slept in your arms."

It's true. I can't even lie about it anymore. To him or anyone else.

I sigh and then roll him onto his back, my body on top of him.

"Shut up about it, Mr. Winslow."

He groans as I grind our hips together.

"Don't make me change my mind about this."

His hips meet my downward thrusts with some of his own.

"You won't. Now that you've had a taste, you won't go back. You need it too much."

"Mm, seems I do. I need it."

"You need *me*."

I pause and then admit. "I need you."

He looks smug beneath me, so I wipe it off his face by sucking his cock down my throat.

It works perfectly.

* * *

At work, I try to remain professional, but it's damn hard when all I want to do is strip my TA down and fuck him.

Or have him fuck me.

I wouldn't mind bending over this desk of mine and letting him stick his dick inside of me. I even may have snuck some lube inside of my bag just in case the opportunity presents itself.

"What are you thinking?" Everly asks, his voice low as he closes the door after office hours are over.

I adjust my tie and meet his gaze.

"Nothing we need to discuss here."

I hear the snick of a lock and his eyes flash mischievously.

"Absolutely not," I tell him as he stalks toward me.

"Nothing bad, just a kiss," he says gently.

Alright, well, a kiss is fine. Totally not inappropriate. Everyone kisses. I even saw Dr. Brown kiss his wife the other day when she visited.

It's not a big deal.

I pull Everly onto my lap and our mouths meet. My tongue snakes into his mouth, licking every corner of him and devouring his taste. By the time we finally pull away, we're both panting.

Hm, maybe not that appropriate, but still. Worth it.

"I can't wait to get home tonight," he says, his cheeks red, his fingers dragging down my heaving chest.

"Can't wait either," I say and rub my nose against his. "Now off you go, Mr. Winslow. Stop trying to get me fired."

He kisses me again, just a peck, and then moves toward the door, adjusting his cock as he goes.

"When I get home from work, I want you prepped and ready," he says.

His words set a fire off inside of me.

"And where exactly do you want me?"

"On the couch, ass out, waiting for me to walk through the door."

The idea of it sets me ablaze, and I nod.

"Fine."

"Good," he grins and then winks, leaving without another word.

Fuck professionalism, I chant in my head as I begin to answer emails. No one needs to know about this.

This is just between him and me.

Chapter Fifteen

Everly

I can't believe this is my life. I can't believe that as soon as I walk through that door, I'll find Silas there waiting for me.

I inhale deeply and rub at my chest. I just need to get in there and fuck him, but goddamn, I'm worried for myself here. I'm worried that I like this guy more than I expected to. I never thought I'd do romance, but here I am, doing it.

I stare down at the flowers in my hand and debate tossing them into the trash, but I bought them on a whim. I wanted to do this.

Shit, if I start serenading him, I will have to give up my man card.

Fucking Silas, making me eat all my words, making me rethink and reshape my beliefs.

I want romance and I want it with him.

I pull out the key he gave me and let myself in, the bouquet of flowers still clutched in my hand. The room is dimly lit and yet my eyes immediately fall to Silas.

Bent over the couch, his ass out, his dark eyes peering over his shoulder at me.

"Hey, hottie," I say, feeling my cheeks heat as I stare at him. My heartbeat triples, and I feel my entire body warm.

Damn, this man has gotten me so good.

I don't even know why. I can't explain what he's done to me.

But he's sure done something with that scowl and that grumpy demeanor. How he always says that he's not going to do something and then does it anyways. He's a walking contradiction, and I'm half in love with him for it.

"Did you bring me flowers?" he asks, still not moving from his place bent over the couch.

"I did," I say and then wet my lips.

"You trying to romance me, Mr. Winslow?"

"You know it," I say, setting them down on the small table before striding toward him. I'll make sure to put them in water before we go to bed. I don't want them wilting on me.

"But romancing can wait because goddamn, look at you," I say, my voice going all raspy when I take in how hot he is. Goddamn, I'm a lucky man. So glad I got to him before LoveJoy could entice him with those ribbons.

The tips of his ears turn pink as he turns his gaze forward and arches his hips up slightly.

"Eager for it, huh?" I say as I start to strip. My clothes fall to the floor as I advance, and as soon as my hands land on his hips, I see that the fish tank has been covered up. Good choice, Silas. Good fucking choice. We don't need a dramatic fish ruining this for us.

"I mean, I wouldn't say I'm eager," Silas replies with a huff. "I'm a grown man. I have patience."

But even as he says it, he wiggles that ass, trying to get me to hurry up. Pfft, he has the patience of a gnat.

It's fucking glorious.

Full Service

My cock weeps as I drag it along his crack, loving the way he grumbles his impatience.

"You're such a liar," I say as I slide a finger into him, testing out how wet he really is. It slips in easily, which means he's prepped well. I don't need to do anything but push my dick inside of him. Not that I do. I want to tease him until he's full-on grumpin' at me. I want him to scowl and demand I give it to him.

"I'm not a liar. I'm the most truthful being on the planet."

I scoff at that and then slap his ass with my free hand, my finger still working in and out of him.

"Did you just spank me?" he gasps, and I grin, doing it again. The sound of my palm bouncing off his ass cheek makes me hornier than I ever thought I could be. But then again, Silas just does things to me.

All the parts of me.

My cock and my heart.

"You were being a bad boy. You deserved it," I say and then spank him a third time.

He gasps and turns his gaze over his shoulder to glower at me.

"I'm not a boy."

"Hm, but wouldn't you say you're my boy?"

"I am thirty-five."

"Thirty-six," I correct him, and his lips turn down further.

"Thank you for reminding me," he grunts, and I half-expect him to move away in frustration, but instead, he just wiggles his butt, enticing me.

"Anytime, old man. Still have a nice body for being near death," I tell him, and he huffs a laugh.

"Even in my prime, I looked nothing like you," he says, his gaze raking over me.

My head grows ten times too big for my body at his words. "Aw, you mean it?"

"You know exactly how good you look, Mr. Winslow. Now fuck me."

I eye that ass, that hole, and wet my lips.

"I think I'd like to tease you a little longer."

"I will riot."

"But I do love a grumpy Silas."

He grumbles under his breath, which only makes me harder. He has no idea what he does to me. He has no fucking clue.

"Then do I need to take what I want?" he asks, standing up and turning around.

Well, hell. I didn't consider this. I bite down on my bottom lip, taking him in. His lithe runner's body, that forearm full of tattoos—which I found out has depth and meaning, the dark scruff on his jaw, his mussed hair.

And then that cock.

Thick and long.

His hands fall on my chest, and I let out a desperate breath as his fingernails drag down to my stomach.

"I can take what I want."

"Will you?" I ask, and he nods, pushing into me, our bodies now flush with each other.

"Do I need to prove it to you?"

I mean, he should. He should so prove it, but then again, I want to fuck him over the couch—been imagining it all day. But the thought of him pushing me down on the sofa and riding me is also a delicious scenario.

"I mean, everything is just a hypothesis until proven, right?"

I have no idea what I'm saying at the moment because his one hand is wrapped around my dick and the other is around my balls, rolling them in his palm.

"A hypothesis is usually made on limited evidence and requires further investigation."

"Sex investigation," I murmur as he leans up and presses his lips to mine.

"Yes, sex investigation. Sextigation."

"Yes, we should create a new major at the university with this knowledge. I bet you'd have record enrollment," I reply as he tugs my dick and leads me toward the front of the couch. When I'm right where he wants me, he shoves me down, my ass and back landing on the cushions. He follows me down, his thighs straddling my hips, his hard dick straining out from his body.

"I think we should resume our research, don't you, Mr. Winslow?"

"Yeah, Dr. Sinclair. I think we should. For science."

He grins down at me and then I feel the head of my cock slot at his hole and a second later, he slams down. I arch up off the couch in shock.

Jesus. He took me in one fell swoop. He didn't even work me in.

"Goddamnit!" I shout and look up to see Silas's head thrown back, his chest heaving.

"God yes," he says, his eyelids fluttering. "Fuck yes."

My fingers dig into his hips and flex roughly when he drags his hole up my entire length and slams down onto me once more. I shout again, the tight ring of his ass strangling my cock.

Oh god, I'm not going to last. I'm going to come embarrassingly fast.

His hips snap up and then down, his pace frantic and wild, making me nearly shoot off the sofa in response. It's too much, too good.

"I think," he heaves, his voice nearly breathless. "I think we need a lot more research to prove our hypothesis."

"Yes," I say in agreement. It's all I can do to get a word out. I'm already half lost, half crazed, half out of my mind. I can't even math anymore. Numbers don't make sense.

Nothing makes sense.

Silas's hands move up his chest and into his hair as he impales himself on me over and over again, until I'm strung tight, my entire body coiled up and ready to snap. Fuck, the picture he makes. The sensuality of it all.

I've never had sex with someone like this. Never had it feel this good.

That's all I know.

It's all I fucking know and that's good enough for me.

I come on a roar, my cock shoved so far up inside of him that he cries out, his body shaking atop me.

"Oh fuck," I grunt as I writhe under him, letting him wring every last drop out of me. Then I look meekly up at him, and he meets my gaze.

"I wasn't done."

"Yeah, about that," I say, grabbing on to his dick and stroking it. "I wasn't either. That was just foreplay."

He arches an eyebrow at me in disbelief.

"Now who's the liar?" he asks, and I shrug.

"Give me two minutes, and I will rock your world."

He cocks his head and then leans down toward me, his lips brushing mine sweetly.

"Oh, Mr. Winslow, you already did. But I'll take a round two. I'll always take more from you."

Jesus fucking Christ, this man.

I thread my fingers through his hair and kiss him deeply, our tongues sliding against each other. My cock is still inside him and when it starts to thicken, Silas groans at the sensation, the sound reverberating through me.

I swallow it all, inhale it.

Full Service

I plan on keeping my word.
Gonna rock his world.

* * *

Silas is on his hands and knees, my cock shuttling in and out of his hole, taking him for another ride. Only this time, instead of riding me, he's bent over the couch like he was when I walked through the door. We've come full circle now.

"That's it," I say, feeling like a god. We've been going at it for literal minutes. At least five. And I'm going like a champ, making him grunt and groan, my name a prayer on his lips.

"That's it, Dr. Sinclair. You take it."

He arches his hips back and does. He takes it so good. I've never had a bottom so fucking good for me. But then again, Silas makes everyone seem dull in comparison.

"And you don't come. Not yet. I'm not through with you."

He grunts his disapproval, which only brings me closer to the edge. I mean, doesn't he realize what those grumpy sounds do to me?

Obviously not because he does it continuously until I'm cross-eyed, my body buried so deep inside of him that I swear I'm going to come out his throat. I lift him by the shoulders until he's standing upright and grab on to the base of his dick as I continue to thrust up into him, feeling his shaft pulse in my hand.

But he can't come. He really can't. I need to sit on it.

"You hold it in," I tell him roughly, my teeth nipping at his earlobe. "You save it for me."

He groans, his head falling back on my shoulder as I use him. And I do. I grind and thrust, canting my hips up furiously until finally, I'm pushed over the edge.

His ass is stuffed full, my cum leaking out of him as he falls forward, his shaking arms holding himself up against the couch.

I don't hesitate, just flip him back onto the couch seat and squirt lube on his cock.

And without any prep, I sink onto his hard length and rock my hips, the sting making me cry out as he splits me open.

But fuck, I love the pain of it.

Love that tomorrow I will wake up and feel what he did to me.

How he destroyed me.

Silas's back is bowed off the couch, his eyes shut as his hands scramble for purchase.

And after one minute of fucking, our hips meeting in loud slaps of skin and sweat, he releases into me, filling my ass up with so much cum that I know I'll be leaking for the rest of the night.

I fall onto him, our sweaty, slick bodies melded together as I nuzzle my face into his neck.

"So, about that sextigation," I say, and Silas huffs a small laugh.

"Still a hypothesis. Still need to collect more data."

"Agreed," I say as his cock slips from my hole. I feel his release drip from me as I wiggle on top of him, loving when his hands come around my back and hold me close, cradling me in his arms.

"We can resume tomorrow. Not at work though."

"Aw, but Dr. Sinclair, there's a lab at the university and I really want to see you in a white lab coat."

"I can arrange that at home."

"With the goggles?"

He rolls his eyes, and I lean up and kiss him.

"And with safety gloves and a beaker. I want the entire setup."

Full Service

He laughs and then rolls us onto our sides, his body pressed against mine.

"That, Everly, can most assuredly be arranged."

Chapter Sixteen

Silas

Well, I didn't realize I could be so happy. Who knew that I just needed an Everly in my life to make me smile? My mouth doesn't know what to do with itself. It positively hurts.

But maybe I'm getting ahead of myself. It's only been a few weeks since this all started, but fuck, it's all gotten so much more intense since he moved in and started sleeping in my bed. I love coming home and knowing that I'll get to see him. Even if it's just for a little while late at night.

Some days he works late at the club, and I end up dozing, trying to wait up for him. But when he has those late nights, he sneaks in and slips into bed beside me, pressing kisses to my shoulders and neck.

How I ever thought I could keep this professional is beyond me.

Everly is addicting.

I would snort him like a drug if I could.

"How about we go away this weekend?" Everly suggests.

"We could go to Monterey Bay and go skinny dipping in the sea."

"I can't. I have plans," I say, feeling my stomach drop at the missed opportunity. No, I wish I could go away this weekend, but sadly this weekend I have that ungodly ribbon dance with Lee. I can't cancel on him. I just fucking can't do that to him. He's been so looking forward to this.

God knows why.

He probably enjoys seeing me blush.

"Aw, what are you doing instead? Can I come?"

"Absolutely not," I mutter. "You are forbidden from coming anywhere near it."

I will not have Everly see me on stage waggling ribbons around my head. That is too unhinged and so damn mortifying. I will never live it down.

"Why not?" he asks, leaning up on his elbows and staring down at me as we lie in bed. He positively glows in the dim light of my room. Or maybe that's the body glitter he can't ever quite scrape off his skin after a night of pulling his clothes off for a living.

Can't say I disapprove though. I quite like how shimmery he is.

"Why not? Well, for one, it's embarrassing."

His eyes widen. "Is that so? Well, now I want to go even more."

I roll my eyes and pull him down for a kiss, hoping to distract him long enough for him to forget about this damn thing. But of course, he doesn't. He brings it back up again minutes later, causing me to sigh.

"Fine, I'll tell you what it is, but I won't tell you where it will be. I won't have you showing up and witnessing it."

"I mean, this only makes me more intrigued. And I have been known to stalk people I'm interested in."

"Since when?"

"Since I met you."

I feel my chest constrict, and I pull him in for another kiss. Can't help it when it comes to this man, apparently. I'm a weak soul.

Everly sighs and then nuzzles into me. It's addicting. I love how cuddly he is. "Now tell me your dirty little secret, Professor. I need to know or I will die."

I hold my breath for a moment and then blurt, "Fine. I was roped into a ribbon dance with LoveJoy."

His head comes up, and he eyes me. "A ribbon dance? With AlmondJoy. Why is this the first I'm hearing of it?"

"It's not something I like to advertise. This entire thing is the bane of my existence. Every time I think of it I want to die."

"And how is AlmondJoy involved?"

"He is directing this horrific dance that he created while high in the woods. So I'm not dancing *with* him, but I'm doing some kind of coordinated ribbon thing with an older man I met at the grocery store. Don't ask me more. I can't cope with the reality of this. I really can't."

His lips twitch, his eyes alight with something I don't recognize.

"An older man? Should I be jealous?"

"God no. *No*. He could be your grandfather."

"Ah, so if he's a grandpa, why doesn't he ask his family to do it?"

"Well, they flaked, so it was left to me."

"Hm, they sound like real assholes."

"Probably are, to be honest. And to think..."

I cut my train of thought off, but it only makes Everly more curious.

"What? You can't end a sentence like that."

Everly continues to gaze at me, and I sigh. "Fine, he has a

grandson he wants to set me up with. He's always harping on about it, but don't worry, I always refuse." Everly's eyes narrow, and I press a hand to his chest. "Really, Everly, I won't be seeing Junior no matter how much Lee begs me to."

Everly bites his bottom lip and glances away from me.

"Junior? Hm. Has a nice ring to it."

I sense the insecurity on his face and cup his cheeks gently. "Really. Don't you worry. I'm not interested in that man. I've never met him and don't plan on it. Not at all."

"But you never know. He could be devastatingly handsome. All your dreams come true."

Well, that's impossible, I think. Because the only man of my dreams is right here on top of me. Not that I say that. Everly is young, impossible to tie down. I will not be scaring him off with grand propositions and feelings when I just got him.

Fuck no.

I'm going to keep him as long as I can by staying quiet.

Until he finds out that boring and stable isn't what he wants.

Then I'll deal with the broken heart, lick my wounds, and move on.

"I'm happy here with you," I reply and then roll us over until I'm straddling him. He blinks up at me, my hands sliding down his chest until my fingers curl under the waistband of his boxer briefs.

"You sure?"

"I'm fucking sure. Now forget about ribbon dances. I would very much like to pretend that it never happened."

He nods up at me and rolls his lips between his teeth. "I can do that."

"Good because we have more important matters to discuss."

He raises an eyebrow as I scoot down his body, my mouth right at his crotch. I pull the fabric of his boxers down and stare at his weeping cock.

"Very important oral matters."

"Oral matters are very dire," he agrees, and I let out a laugh.

"I think so too. It would be so unethical to ignore this."

"So unethical."

* * *

The day leading up to the ribbon dance sours my mood more than it should. By the time I enter Lee's residence at the retirement home and see him decked out in hot pants, I nearly keel over and die. My heart can't cope with this.

I'm in a near state of panic. I can feel my heartbeat in my eyeballs.

"I refuse to do this, Lee," I hiss as I come to a stop, trying not to look at his bare legs in those bright pink shorts. "Absolutely refuse. If you make me, I will never bring you to the diner to get french fries again."

"Pfft, stop being ridiculous. You're here. You're doing it. Now change into these."

He hands me a pair of bright purple shorts that are far too short, and I shake my head.

"Fuck no."

"Sun's out. Bun's out," he says with a clap of his hands and a high-pitched cackle. "And when you get changed, LoveJoy will be by to help us put on ribbons. They're even color-coordinated with our outfits."

"Good fuck," I murmur as I take the shorts from him.

"And where is the shirt, Lee? Hm?"

"No shirt. Just ribbons."

"Good God. I want to die," I grumble as I move into the bathroom and change. There's no point in arguing. Lee knows this. I know this, but when I catch a look at myself in the mirror, I clasp my hands in front of my crotch and squeal.

"Lee! These are more than buns out! My balls are dangling."

"Oh, really? Show me," he says, and I peer out of the bathroom at him.

"There is no way I can wear these out in public. This is indecent."

"Well, how can I decide if they are if you hide in there?"

I glower at him and watch as his eyes positively twinkle. "Fine, Lee, you pervert. You want to see my nuts. Go right ahead."

I step out and let them dangle. Like ornaments on a tree.

Lee giggles and slaps a hand over his eyes. "Good lord, boy. Put those away."

"I don't think I will!" I reply, feeling defiant now. Maybe I should make sure everyone sees my balls. Maybe this is what they get.

A ball sac ribbon dance.

"Silas!" Lee says with a wheeze. "Change those shorts. You are going to scare everyone away."

"Good. Let them see my goods. You bought me these shorts and insisted I wear them. This is your fault."

"It was a joke."

"Yes, well, joke's on you, old man. I quite like them," I lie. "I just need the ribbons to complete the outfit. I can put some on my balls too."

"Do not do that!" Lee says with another wheeze.

"I will!"

Lee's face is red, tears streaming down his face.

"You wouldn't."

But oh, I will. I'm fully committed now. Damnable Lee and his silly shorts.

LoveJoy is thrilled with this new development though. Of course he is. He's not bothered at all by the fact that when he appears, I ask him, straight-faced, to put ribbons on my privates.

He grins widely and waggles his eyebrows.

"Fabulous! I love your imagination. And I love the shorts. Very indecent, Dr. Sinclair."

I frown at him, hating that he's reminding me that I'm a professor and should most definitely not be prancing around in hot pants with ribbons on my balls, but here we are.

It's not like my students hang out with these old people.

I can wear my ribbons with dignity.

"Yes, I'm very imaginative. That's me."

LoveJoy grins widely at me. "Wonderful. Now let me decorate the rest of your body with these. You two are going to make waves."

"I hope I drown," I say, watching as LoveJoy attaches ribbons to my arms and legs, and when he gets to my balls, I just roll my eyes to the ceiling and let him have at it.

* * *

I have made a terrible mistake. A huge, no-good mistake by letting LoveJoy tie these ribbons to my balls. I shouldn't have been so stubborn, but here I am, waiting to go on stage with Lee and regretting all my life choices.

"I need to go back and change out of these," I say, the ribbons tickling my inner thighs as they blow in the slight breeze from the open windows.

"You can't. We go on next," Lee says, pulling a comb from the pocket of his walker and brushing it through his hair.

"Good lord," I murmur and wish I could just disappear into the earth.

I'd very much like to sink into the floor and reappear in another time. A time when I'm not enrolled in the ribbon dance and didn't get stubborn and have LoveJoy tie ribbons to my balls.

He enjoyed that far too much.

Really had a lot to say about them.

Apparently, they're very lopsided and in need of a good trimming.

I'll have to ask Everly about this. He will be honest and tell me if they should be examined. Or maybe altered.

Because, quite frankly, if he likes them, then I don't fucking care about anything else.

I feel the beat of the music beneath my feet and the cheering from the crowd. I can't even watch what the others are doing up on stage. The couple performing now is the young woman I met a couple weeks ago and her grandmother. The poor woman just stared at me and sighed as she walked past me to the stage, ribbons in her hair, on her fingers, and her ankles.

I have no idea what she's been doing up there. I haven't been looking.

All I know is that she's most definitely not showing off her lady bits.

"Let's raise the roof for these incredible dancers!" LoveJoy shouts, and the sound of his voice makes my ears ring. Oh god. This is terrible.

I need to run away and hide. But then again, the look of pure joy on Lee's face makes me stay put. He's living for this, for my utter humiliation.

All too soon, the music fades and Lee hops around on his feet. Well, as much as he can hop. And then he's squeaking onto the stage, a bright grin on his face. I follow forlornly, tugging my shorts down as far as I can to hide my balls. No one wants to see them.

Really, they're not that great.

"And now for the stars of the show, the crazy and wild Lee

Full Service

and Silas!" LoveJoy hoots into the mic. He's flapping his arms around, directing all gazes toward us. Garrett is standing in the audience, waving his arms around in a sensual wave, waggling his head to the sound of an upbeat Enya. Everyone is enjoying this more than me.

Every-damn-one.

I close my eyes and feel my nostrils flare just as a round of applause picks up. I'm trying like hell not to glance at the dozens of onlookers, staring at us as the music grows louder.

"Let's make some fucking noise!" Garrett shouts, his words in great contrast to the music currently bellowing through the speakers.

Not that anyone seems to care about the foul language. This is a den of heathens and sinners.

Lee is wiggling around, his head bobbing ferociously, his butt bobbing as he holds onto his walker. And I can't help but join in. Because we rehearsed this. It's only three minutes up here. It's not a big deal in the grand scheme of things.

My arms flap upward and flutter around me, the ribbons whipping around as I move, and close my eyes once more, trying like hell to not think about what I'm doing. But curiosity gets the better of me and I peek an eyeball open, only to see Lee grinding on his walker and immediately shut it once more.

I don't need to see that.

I really don't. Then again, no one needs to see me either. I bet they're all closing their eyes as well. They probably don't want to see the ribbons on my balls and dangling down my thighs.

"Look at that ass!" a voice suddenly shouts from the audience.

My heart stutters, and I stop moving, my eyelids fluttering open. I know that voice.

I fucking know it.

"That's my man! Mine!" he shouts.

My eyes pop open all the way, and there he is.

Everly.

I feel my entire body set aflame at just the mere glimpse of him. If I get a boner on stage, I will have to retreat to the mountains of Tibet and never return.

Fuck, why is he here? How did he find me, and why the fuck is he holding a sign?

One that reads, "Ribbon dancers do it better!"

He grins widely at me and winks.

"Shake that ass, Dr. Sinclair!"

My mouth drops open and my hands cover my groin, trying to hide my balls from him. Which is ridiculous. They were in his mouth earlier. He rolled them around his tongue quite nicely.

When I don't shake my ass like he wants me to, Everly moves through the crowd toward me, hopping on stage with far more coordination than is necessary, and pulls me into him, grinding against me, using those stripper moves that he knows so well. Everyone is screaming now. Even Lee is hooting, throwing ribbons at us while LoveJoy growls lowly into the mic.

It's insanity. This entire thing is ridiculous, but I don't move away. I just stand there as Everly drags his hands down my bare chest and squats, his face *right there*, peeling my hands away from my crotch.

His eyes slash up to mine as he tugs on the ribbons and a sensual pain lances up my thighs.

Fucker. He knows exactly what he's doing.

But before I can tell him off, he spins around and drags his ass up my legs before standing up, his left arm weaving around my neck as he uses me like a pole. I let out a low groan as he plays me like an instrument. And fuck, I don't mind being played.

He can play me all goddamn day.

"Look at that. Two lovebirds grinding on stage! Isn't love grand?" LoveJoy coos, and a second later, the music finally comes to an end. Thank God it's over, despite everyone hollering for more, for an encore.

But I refuse. I won't be on this stupid stage for one more second.

And Everly shouldn't be here. *He shouldn't be here.*

"What are you doing here?" I growl into his ear as he leans back against me, his chest heaving slightly. Like he's run a marathon.

I thought he was more fit than this.

Everly doesn't answer, just spins around and presses a kiss to my lips, right in front of the crowd. It only makes them more feral, hungry for more of a show.

These are horny fuckers, it seems.

"I had to see my boo dancing on stage. The famed and infamous ribbon dance you told me about. I just couldn't miss it."

"How did you know where I was? I never told you. Did you put tracking software on my phone?"

As soon as the words leave my mouth, Lee meanders up and pats me on the back.

"Ah, so I see you two have met, Silas." He pulls Everly into a hug and then turns toward me. "This is Junior."

I blink and blink some more, my brain spinning. What the hell is going on? Who the fuck is Junior?

"Yes, he's my grandson," Lee says with a wide smile. "Seems you two know each other *very* well."

I stare at Lee and then back at Everly, still trying to wrap my mind around it all.

"Did you know about this?" I ask, and Everly shakes his head.

"No, I promise I didn't. I had no idea you were doing the

ribbon dance with my grandpa, until you said something the other day. Then it just clicked."

I glance between them again, trying to see the resemblance, but come up short. I've got nothing. I would have never been able to tell they were related.

"And you didn't tell me when you figured it out?" I ask.

"I wanted to surprise you."

I glower at him, and he pecks a kiss to my nose. Well, I can't be mad when he does *that*.

"But wait, you two have different last names."

"Not really, actually. I'm Everly Winslow-O'Conner. I just shortened it to Winslow on my college applications. The hyphen and apostrophe were too hard."

I scrunch my nose and frown at him. "Too hard?"

"Look, we can discuss this later. Let's get you in some clothes," Everly says. "I don't like everyone seeing your pretty balls. Especially Garrett."

Oh fuck, Garrett's a student. He's seen my balls.

This is not going to end well.

I look over at him and see him wink at me. Oh, fuck me silly.

"Is Garrett going to tell on me?" I ask, and Everly shakes his head.

"No, he's cool. Don't worry. No one will know about this. I promise."

I sigh and let him lead me off stage, Lee following behind. As we move, people clap us on the back and whistle, but I barely hear it, barely feel it. I'm just amazed that Everly showed up here, that he's Lee's grandson.

What are the fucking chances of that?

I can't quite comprehend it. This is like some kind of ridiculous movie, the kind I hate so much.

When we're back in Lee's room, Everly hugs his grandpa before pulling me into the bathroom and shutting the door.

Full Service

As soon as it clicks shut, the air is sucked out of the small space. It's just me and him, the two of us breathing heavy together in the small space.

"Okay, so as ridiculous as that was, you looked so fucking hot up there," Everly says at the same time I blurt, "I can't believe you saw that."

We grin at each other, and he takes a step closer to me. What little air is left evaporates right out of the room. All I can sense, all I can feel is him.

"It was so worth it. That was three minutes of utter sex," Everly says as my cheeks redden.

"You must have been hallucinating. That was three minutes of pure humiliation."

"Nah, I got to see ribbons on your balls. I take that as a win."

He's flush with me now, his lips trailing across my neck, his hand snaking between my legs and sliding down my shorts. He cups my balls, his fingers gingerly touching the ribbon tied loosely there.

"Let me see it," he whispers, and I groan in acceptance. "Say it. Say I can see."

"Yeah. Yes. Okay." It's all I can do to formulate words when he's touching me like that.

He bites at my neck before tugging my shorts down and stepping away.

And there they are, my lopsided balls with glittering ribbons trailing across my thighs.

"Fuck, that's hot. I didn't know ribbons would do it for me, but they so do."

He kneels before me and rubs his face across my cock. His fingers tug on the ribbons gently, making my balls sway between my legs, like pendulums in a clock.

"When I get you home, I'm gonna suck your dick and then fuck your ass."

The way he says it, those inappropriate words, makes my cock leak.

"Who says I'm going to let you fuck my ass?"

"Me. I say so."

He grins up at me and my fingers trail over his cheeks and into his hair.

"Fine, if you insist," I grunt as he kisses the tip of me before loosening the ribbons and tucking them in his pocket.

He pushes himself up and meets my gaze. "But we're not doing anything right now. Grandpa will never let us live it down."

He presses his forehead against mine and pulls my body against his. I'm completely naked against him now, my skin scraping against the fabric of his clothes. I want him bare as well, want to feel that warm, smooth skin against mine.

But he's right. We can't. We can't do anything now.

"I can't believe you're Junior. I can't believe that he's been trying to set me up with you this entire time."

"I know. It's fucking nuts, right? He did mention an older man he met. But I told him I wasn't interested."

I scoff and arch my cock against his. It's hard, needy, just like mine.

"Of course you weren't. I'm sure Lee told you how boring I am. It put you off."

"You're anything but boring, Dr. Sinclair. You're so fucking opposite of boring I don't know what to do with all the excitement inside of me right now."

I huff a laugh at that. He couldn't be more wrong. I'm not exciting in the least, but fuck, if he thinks so, then so be it.

"But to be honest, I wasn't interested in this random man because I was interested in you. Have been for quite a while."

When he says things like that, it makes my heart fluttery. It gives me wings.

Full Service

I could fly, soar. Don't tie me down, Earth. Let me live.

"Come on. Let me get you your clothes and then let's go take Grandpa out for some food. All that gyrating up on stage probably made him hungry."

I nod and then hold on to him a little tighter when he tries to leave. I don't want him to move away from me. But eventually he has to. He extricates himself from my arms and makes his way out of the bathroom, only to return a moment later with my clothes. I hurriedly pull them on before stepping out, seeing a fully clothed Lee as well.

Thank fuck for that. I never want to see another pair of hot pants or ribbons again in my life.

"Junior said something about lunch. I'm famished," Lee says with a knowing grin. "I'm sure you are too. All that sexual tension looming."

Everly beams over at me and sends me a knowing wink.

"Plus, I need all the gossip on how you two got together," Lee adds.

Everly pulls my hand to his mouth and kisses my knuckles.

"We'll tell you everything," he says with a grin.

Chapter Seventeen

Everly

Grandpa is munching happily on his french fries when we explain how everything went down between Silas and me.

"I was just irresistible," I say, and Silas glares at me. Love that frown, all sexy and grumpy.

"You were tolerable," he replies. "And always in my space. You seduced me with sweet coffees."

"I seduced you with my ass. Let's be honest."

Silas shifts in his seat and nudges me. "Do not say things like that around Lee."

"Why not?" I ask, watching as my grandpa grins at me, a bit of french fry stuck to his bottom lip. He doesn't bother with it, just wears it confidently.

"Because he will get ideas in his head. Did you know he asked me about snowballing men?"

I choke on my soda as a laugh erupts out of me. "Grandpa, seriously?"

Cora Rose

He shrugs, looking pleased as pie. "What? I didn't know what it meant. You youngins are filthy."

"I mean, filthy is fun. Right, Silas?"

"I refuse to answer that. Refuse."

I can't help the chuckle that slips out of me.

"Either way, the point is moot. He's my TA, Lee. Nothing can come of this."

My mood instantly plummets. I don't know what he's going on about. We are absolutely going to make something come of this. Besides me, of course.

And him.

He comes a lot.

It's quite perfect, actually.

"We're living together," I blurt.

Grandpa stops chewing and eyes us both. "Is that so? That's a new fact that no one cared to tell me. I can't believe you moved my grandson in and didn't tell me, Silas."

Silas looks a little guilty, sinking down in his seat slightly.

"Yes, well, I didn't know he was your grandson. Why do you call him Junior, anyways?"

"Well, my name is Everly too. Lee for short. So he's Junior," my grandpa explains.

"Well, that makes entirely too much sense. But back to the situation at hand. Your grandson was in a bit of an emergency," Silas continues. "Did you know, Everly has been living in a hovel run by some warlord? His roof caved in with the storm."

Oh well, shit. I didn't want Grandpa to know about *that*.

"Is that true?"

"Yes, but Gramps, really, it's fine. Silas saved the day. Please don't worry. And please don't tell Dad. I don't need him worrying."

Silas seems to finally understand what he's done and he sits up slightly, adjusting the buttons on his shirt.

Full Service

"Yes, Lee. It's fine. Don't worry. Everly's in good hands."

I am. In very good and sexy hands. And I plan on making sure it stays that way. Silas may say there is nothing to be done about this, but he doesn't know how well I stick.

Grandpa eyes us both and then claps his hands together loudly, making me jump. "Well, that's good news. I expect wedding details within the month."

"Fuck off," Silas mutters, and I place my arm around his shoulders.

"Yeah, don't worry. You'll totally be invited. Maybe you could walk me down the aisle."

Grandpa gets teary-eyed at that, and I swallow roughly. It was a bit of a joke, but now that I say it, I can see it. I can imagine the way Silas would look in a proper suit, standing at the end of the aisle, watching me approach. Or maybe I'd be the one waiting. Maybe he'd walk down the aisle toward me.

I don't know, never thought about marriage before.

But for some reason, with Silas, it just clicks.

It makes total sense.

I can envision everything crystal clear.

* * *

"You shouldn't have given Lee hope," Silas says as soon as we're back at his place, the door shut, the lights turned on.

I shrug and pull my sweatshirt off, tossing it onto the couch, and then toe off my shoes.

"Meh, it's fine. I mean, would it be the worst to marry me?" I eye him and watch as Silas's eyes swivel down my chest, landing on the zipper of my jeans.

His tongue peeks out and he wets those pink, plump lips.

"It would be terrible. Terrible for my health."

"Yeah, okay, old man. What if I'm good for your health? I rejuvenate you."

Silas huffs and takes a step toward me. "You do offer a variety of cardio options."

"I'm very good for your heart."

Not sure if he's good for mine, to be honest. He isn't taking this whole thing very seriously. But to be fair, I haven't been taking it seriously either. Not until today. When I saw him up there on stage, shaking that ass just to make my grandpa happy, I knew I wanted more than just casual.

Not sure if he feels the same way though.

I've never had my heart broken before. I don't want to start now. Seems quite dull and boring, really.

"You are very, very good for my heart," Silas says, his breath hitting my cheek as he runs his nose along my jaw. "You make it pound so incredibly fast. It's like running a marathon. I'll have a six-pack by the time this is done."

I groan as his fingers push into my hair, his lips meeting mine. Our tongues tangle, the two of us grinding up against each other until I finally pull away.

"I... Oh god, Silas. You're so fucking hot. But wait. *Wait*."

He clutches me to him, his fingers digging into my skin, almost trying to pull me into him, but I resist. Suddenly needing to know. I need to know.

"What is it?" he asks, his voice rough.

I suddenly feel nervous, adrift. How the hell do I bring this up? What the hell do I say?

"What..." I wet my lips nervously. "What are we?"

Silas's eyes darken and his fingers tighten on me.

"We?"

"Yeah, you know...this. What is this?"

"Sex," he says, his eyes meeting mine. "A lot of sex."

For some reason, that doesn't delight me to no end like it

should. I love sex, don't get me wrong, but I want this to be more. Never in my life have I wanted more, until now.

"What's wrong? What's with that face?" he asks.

"Nothing. It's... I was hoping for more."

"More?"

He looks genuinely perplexed. That's not a good sign. I know I don't scream commitment, but fuck, shouldn't he want to keep me? Even just a little bit?

"Yeah. More."

Our words are soft and swirl around us, seeming to confuse the fuck out of Silas in the process. He looks almost dizzy.

"Right now, Everly...right now this can only be sex. You're my TA."

Well, that makes no sense. None. Not one rational thing about the words coming out of his mouth.

"So, we can have sex, but that's all it can be?"

He clears his throat. "Yes."

"That's not logical."

Silas's eyes whip up to meet mine. "How so?"

"I mean, you're worried about getting caught, right? Like what will happen if they find out we're fucking?"

He nods, clipped and concise.

"So, what does it matter if we're together then?"

His left eye twitches and his bottom lip is pulled between his teeth.

"I see your point."

"Yeah, I have the best points."

"I guess we're already fucking, it doesn't really matter if we're...more."

My heart rate triples. "Exactly. More."

"More won't necessarily get me fired. Sitting on your dick will."

"Yeah, but no one is getting fired. We'll behave. We'll be

basically saints on campus. No one needs to know you're my boyfriend."

Silas huffs a small laugh. "Ah, so more is boyfriends then?"

"Yeah. I think so. It makes sense."

He hums lowly and then pulls me in for a long-drawn-out kiss.

"Fine then," he mutters. "Time for you to fuck your boyfriend now. Let's make it official."

"Hell yes."

***

Being Silas's boyfriend is fucking hard.

He makes me so goddamn hard.

I sit in the biology lecture and am hard. Then I go to his office hours to work with students and end up miserable because I'm hard again.

All I want to do is bend him over the desk and take him right then and there. I don't want to wait until we're home. I said we'd be good, and I have been. I've been so good. For weeks I've behaved, been the most upstanding boyfriend in North America, but now I'm starting to crack.

I'm starting to lose my fucking mind.

I want him all the time.

I want to hold him, kiss him, fuck him.

How can everyone not see how I've been feeling? It's obvious. Anyone who looks once at me can see that I have heart-eyes only for him.

It's more than sex too. It's how we talk to each other, how I share my dreams and worries, how he does the same. I want a future with him.

I want to marry him.

And that thought makes me hard again.

"Honestly, can you at least try to behave?" Silas whispers when he catches me drooling over the sight of him. I mean, how am I supposed to behave when he looks so goddamn good in a knit sweater?

They should be illegal.

Yarn should be banned from college campuses.

"It's hard to when my boyfriend looks so good."

Silas grumbles at me, his cheeks flushing. "Behave."

A low moan slips from me. When he gets all professor-y on me I can't help but get even more turned on.

"I'm having a biological emergency."

"Then go take care of it before class starts."

"I think I need your help."

Silas straightens his sweater and side-eyes me. "Fine. You have five minutes."

I nod and stride out of the lecture hall, almost running at this point. When I make it to his office, I wait impatiently for him to unlock it. As soon as we step through the threshold and the door is closed, I'm on him.

I can't help it.

"Everly," Silas hisses as my lips attack his. "*Everly*."

"Babe. I'm so fucking turned on right now. I can't think. All my blood is in my dick."

I grind it up against him so he can feel what he does to me.

"It's this sweater. I never knew I liked yarn on men, but I so do."

He chuckles as I kiss my way across his jaw and then drop to my knees.

"Let me suck your dick. We have two minutes and we both know you only last one."

Silas grumps above me.

"I can last quite a while, just so you know."

I do know. He can come multiple times too. But right now, I

just want to suck his dick and then sit in that class, listening to him speak, watching his mouth move, edging myself into oblivion.

"We said we wouldn't do this," Silas says, but his dick is already in my mouth and I'm swallowing him whole. I can't really speak about this at the moment and honestly, having him in my mouth is such a relief that I don't even care that I'm breaking all the rules.

If he got fired, would it really be so bad?

Then we could travel around the States and fuck and be out in the open like a normal couple. We wouldn't have to hide away like we are. It's driving me nuts, seeing him and not being able to have him.

I want to shout it to the world that he's my boyfriend.

But this is all I get, for now.

"Fuck. Fuck," Silas grunts and then he's unloading into my mouth, his legs jerking as he comes.

When I finally pull off his cock, I stare up at him.

"That was really fast," I say with a grin, and Silas tucks himself away.

"Yes, well, we're in a rush. I can't be blamed."

He takes a step back from me and helps me stand. My dick is straining out from my pants, and I stare forlornly at it.

"I can't help you, Mr. Winslow," Silas says with a small smirk. "I really do need to get back to class, but thank you for your assistance."

I roll my eyes and peck a kiss to his lips.

"You're welcome. I'll take what I need from you when I get home."

"Fair. When will you be home?" he asks, his hand moving to the doorknob. It's only as he twists it that we both realize it wasn't locked. Anyone could have come in and seen me on my knees for him.

"Late. I have a late shift."

"Hm, well, I won't wait up then," he says and then his eyes darken. "But feel free to fuck me awake."

Oh, I so fucking will.

"And Everly," he says as he pulls the door open. I crane my neck toward him, and he lowers his voice. "Next time, lock the fucking door."

Chapter Eighteen

Silas

I've been roped into a beach cleanup, one of the worst places on Earth—with all the sand and the wind and the people.

But I said yes to attending because Everly looked so damn cute when he asked me, peering down at me as his cock softened inside of my ass. I was basically coerced into saying yes to this. I would have probably died if I said no.

"Come on, look alive," Everly says, nudging me softly.

I really need to not reach out and hold his hand. Students are here and so is the department chair. I need to behave and keep my hands to myself.

It's hard though when your boyfriend looks delicious.

And so does his ass. I kind of want to eat it behind that big beach umbrella over there. Not that I would. This is not a picnic. We're here to work.

As someone gives instructions, I fold my arms across my chest, trying to look less like a scowling mongrel and more like a happy professor who loves his job.

Fact. I do love my job.

I do not love this.

I stare down the long shoreline and see a bit of driftwood perched in the sand, a woman's gardening hat sitting on top. Hm, why's the wood wearing a hat? What does it mean? Is this symbolic?

I don't know. I don't know if I want to know.

"The seagulls are going to poop on me," I grumble, and Everly turns to look at me.

"Aw, I bet they won't. I come to the beach a lot and have never been pooped on."

He spoke too soon though because a moment later, a bird lands a fat one right on his shirt. He opens his mouth in shock and then laughs.

"Well, fuck."

"Yes, they're angry air missiles, shitting and stealing food. Combine that with the sand and the wind, this is basically hell."

"You're a biology professor. You're supposed to love the beach and all creatures."

"I'm not a marine biologist. I just like the way organisms work. Behind a microscope. This is not my jam. There's a reason I quit being the biology club advisor."

I use my tongs to pick up a used condom and frown. "And neither is this. Have you gotten your recent Hep B vaccine? I really need you to reassure me right now."

Just as Everly opens his mouth to respond, I feel something wet land on my arm. I stare down at the white poop saturating my skin and nearly peel it off to escape this.

"There is bird shit on my arm, Everly."

He's grinning, a snort escaping his parted lips.

"Oh my god."

"They're out to get me. Things with wings should not exist."

Everly's eyes are watering and he's trying like hell not to

start rolling around on the ground. If he touches the sand and it gets in his hair, he's sleeping on the balcony. I refuse to have miniscule dead fossils in my bed.

Refuse.

I'm not a caveman.

"Seems they like us. Maybe they're marking us in some way."

"No, they hate that we're here," I say and then blow a raspberry at them. They squawk in response, and I threaten them with a discarded plastic cup.

"I'll leave this for you to choke on, you fucks!" I hiss and then take a deep breath, not wanting anyone to think I'm serious. As much as I hate these winged devils, I don't really want them to consume plastic. It is very sad what's happened to the beach, and I am impressed that Everly spends his free time out here picking up trash.

But I honestly would rather be buried deep in his ass or kissing him than standing out here, getting pooped on.

This is not sexy at all.

"Let me get you something to wipe that off with," Everly says and as he strides off, I can't help but gaze at his ass. It's hard not to. It's basically a national treasure at this point. They should display it in the Louvre.

I'd sure as hell pay to stare at it.

I hear snickers and turn to look at some students who've been watching me. My eyebrows lower, and I glower at them.

"Do you need something?" I ask, and they quickly glance away, whispering to themselves.

I really need to keep my eyes to myself.

Just as I think that, Everly appears with a wipe and helps me mop the shit up. When he finishes, Dr. Brown makes an appearance, clapping me on the shoulder.

"Nice of you to show up, Dr. Sinclair."

I wince and nod. "Anything for the environment. I love the beach."

Dr. Brown grins at me, and I know he knows I'm lying. It's no secret that I don't like sand or waves or the gulls.

"Seems so," Dr. Brown says and then eyes Everly. "And you even brought your TA?"

His eyes swivel across Everly, taking him in, and I nod. "Yes. He's been very helpful this year."

Very helpful in finding my prostate and making me cum hands-free.

And also being sweet and buying me flowers and holding me while I fall asleep.

"Yes, well he is a bright and shining star."

That he is, especially when he's moaning my name, but I choke that thought down. I do not need to accidentally let that slip from my lips. No siree.

"Alright, well, I'll let you get back to collecting trash, and I'll see you after."

"Can't wait," I mumble and then turn back to the task at hand.

And I really do focus, for a long while. I fill up an entire trash bag, all while getting sand in my shoes. The entire time, I don't look at Everly, but then I make the mistake of doing it and regret it. Because now I want to kiss him. I want to lick his face and then his ass.

I want to do all the things to him.

But of course I can't do that. Dr. Brown is here and a whole bunch of students. I absolutely cannot.

Even if he is my boyfriend.

And even if I really, really want to.

"Mr. Winslow," I say lowly, trying to play it cool. It's hard to do when I'm overheating though, and my dick is poking into the plastic bag I'm holding in front of me.

Full Service

"Yes, Dr. Sinclair?" Everly replies.

"I think there is a large mountain of trash behind that umbrella over there."

"Yeah?" he asks, craning his neck to the right.

"It's quite large. I saw a sea turtle meander over to it. Had a straw up its nose."

"Oh shit," he says and sets everything down and strides purposefully toward that umbrella that's sticking out at an angle from the sand.

I'm going to hell. Sorry turtles and straw lovers everywhere. But really, can you blame me? I just need a taste. Just a little taste to get me through this hell.

"I don't see a turtle, Silas," Everly says, his eyes wide as his head swivels side to side.

"There's no turtle. Unless you count the one in my pants."

Everly's lips twitch up. "Why, Dr. Sinclair, is there a turtle in your pants?"

"You'll have to find out," I say lowly and then take a step toward him. No one can see us behind here. This umbrella is as big as the state of Maine. I have approximately one minute to get what I need.

I pull Everly into me and kiss him roughly, my tongue sneaking into his mouth.

He groans as I grind my hips up against him, feeling his cock lengthen down his thigh as I do so.

"I can't wait to get off this godforsaken beach and fuck you," I whisper, and Everly groans into my mouth once more.

"Why are you so hot, so irresistible?"

"God made me this way, just so I could tempt you."

I groan because he's right. If there is a god, he made Everly just for me.

As my tongue slips into his mouth once more, I hear a gasp

and then a sigh. I quickly pull away from Everly, my entire body heating.

Oh my god.

Someone saw us.

I peel my eyelids open and crane my neck to the side.

"Dr. Sinclair, Everly," Dr. Brown says, and I feel my stomach drop to my feet.

Oh hell. My department chair just saw me kissing and grinding up against my TA. I'm done for. I may as well walk right into the sea at this point. It's over.

"Excuse me. There was something on his tongue," I lie.

Yes, my tongue was on his. Nothing more, nothing less.

Dr. Brown arches an eyebrow at me, and I glance away.

"It was very dire indeed. A biological emergency."

Dr. Brown's other eyebrow rises. At this point, he's going to levitate off the ground if I keep lying to him.

"Seems like quite the hazard. Are you alright, Everly?" Dr. Brown asks, probably wondering if I was sexually harassing him. Of course it looks like I was. He's a student, my TA. I should be ashamed of myself.

I'm three percent ashamed of myself. For getting caught.

"I'm fine. Great even. Dr. Sinclair was super helpful."

Dr. Brown does not seem appeased, and fuck, I need to leave before I end up in the sand hyperventilating. I may end up inhaling those itty bitty little bits of fossils and garnering a new, unheard of disease. I may have my eyeballs plucked out by the seagulls.

I can't stay here.

"Well then. Excuse me," I say and then push past Dr. Brown and the crowd of students, who are gathering to see what all the commotion is. I walk without looking back until I reach my car.

Full Service

With fumbling fingers, I manage to unlock the damnable thing and slip inside, breathing deeply through my nose.

I will not panic.

I will not.

There are worse things that could happen. Much worse.

Like my dick could fall off. Or Everly could die.

Yes, far worse than losing my job.

Oh fuck, I'm going to lose my job.

A knock on the window has me glancing up, and I see Everly standing there, his gaze drawn, his lips turned down in a worried frown.

"Open up," he says, his voice muffled behind the glass.

Reluctantly, I unlock the door and let him slide into the passenger side.

He closes the door and we sit in silence, nothing but the sound of my panicked breathing hitting my eardrums.

"I'm sorry about that," he finally says, and I shake my head, swallowing roughly.

"It's my fault. I should have known better than to do that at the beach."

"No, it's mine. I shouldn't have believed you about the turtle."

It's so fucking ridiculous that I can't help but snort a laugh.

"Not my finest excuse."

"Yeah. Fucking fuck. If I had known what a liar you were, then I wouldn't have let you kiss me like that."

I sigh and rub at my eyes.

"God, Everly. I don't know what to do."

Everly shifts in his seat, and I can feel his eyes on me. "Are we gonna break up?"

I whip my head toward him, my chest constricting. "What?"

"I mean, are you going to break up with me now?"

I wheeze slightly. No way in hell do I want to do that. "Do you think we should?"

He shrugs, biting his lip and turning away slightly. "I mean, I'd get it if you wanted to. I don't want you to lose your job for me."

Doesn't he know? Doesn't he know he's worth more than that?

"No."

He's silent, his breath sucked in, holding it, waiting.

"No. I won't lose you too."

"You sure?" he whispers, and I nod.

"I've never been more sure of anything in my entire life."

I'm nervous, a jittery anxious thing when I make my way onto campus on Monday. I spent the weekend in Everly's arms, fucking him, holding him, letting him console me. We talked through all the possibilities of what may happen and what we'd do if it came down to the worst possible thing.

He held on to me for dear life the entire time, almost as if what happens on Monday could ruin things for us.

But I won't let it.

I fucking won't.

Everly is the best thing to ever happen to me. We can make this work, whatever happens.

I straighten my tie as I make my way to Dr. Brown's office for a meeting to discuss what he saw this weekend. His e-mail sent that evening was curt and short, and I honestly have no idea what to expect.

I was caught with a student, my TA. This won't end well.

My shaking fist raps against the door, and I wait.

Everything is sweating—my pits, my nose, my knees.

"Come in," Dr. Brown says, and I do, stepping into his office and shutting the door behind me.

Dr. Brown looks serious and regal behind his desk, his hands folded tightly as I lower myself into a leather chair.

"Dr. Sinclair," he says with a nod of his head. He's lost all respect for me. I can see it in his eyes, in the way he won't meet my gaze. He doesn't even smile.

"Good morning," I reply and feel my sweaty palms slide against each other as I try to maintain my composure.

"Seems we have something to discuss, as per my email."

I nod and swallow, my throat clicking loudly in the silent room.

"I'm sorry," I croak. "I didn't mean for it to happen."

Dr. Brown leans back in his chair, it creaks under his weight. "I'd assumed as much. You've been nothing but professional the entire time we've worked together. Almost too much."

"I've always tried to be."

"But you slipped up."

I sigh and run a hand down my face. "He's irresistible. I blame him entirely."

Dr. Brown chuckles, and I peer up at him, watching as he smiles.

"I could see that at the beach. The way he looked at you as well. I spoke to him, you know, just to make sure it was consensual. He said it was. Took the blame entirely."

"Yes, well..." I don't know what to say, so I just let my words trail off into nothing. It was his fault entirely. Him and that delicious ass.

"You're probably wondering what we need to do about this."

"Yes. I'm assuming I'm going to be let go."

Dr. Brown is silent for a moment, his mouth slightly parted. "No, Dr. Sinclair. No need for that."

My world stutters and pauses. "What?"

"No need for that. You're not fired. Absolutely not. You're a tenured professor and a damn fine one too. No, we won't say anything about this. Everly is almost graduated. He has a month left. You two will just keep whatever it is between you two and will save any public displays of affection for home."

I shift in my seat anxiously, almost unsure if I'm hearing things correctly.

"What?"

"Do I need to repeat it?"

I shake my head. "No. No. I heard you. I can absolutely do that. We can do that. No problem."

"Please do. I don't want this coming back to bite me in the ass."

I shake my head so hard, my brain rattles in my skull. "It won't. I promise."

Dr. Brown meets my gaze finally, and I see his eyes soften. "Can I be honest with you? I haven't seen you this happy in years."

I feel my eyes sting and grow wet. "I haven't been."

"Then I'm glad we've decided on this. Life is short, Silas. You have to make the best of it."

I nod, my throat clicking.

"I do. And I will. I promise that what happened at the beach won't happen again."

"Be sure of it," he says with a nod.

He reaches across his desk, and I shake his hand.

"You deserve to be happy. Enjoy it."

When I leave his office, I feel my steps grow lighter, almost buoyant. And by the time I arrive home, I'm floating on clouds of air.

* * *

Full Service

"You didn't message me!" Everly nearly shouts when I make my way into our house.

Yes, ours. It's his and mine now.

Everything about this is ours.

I've decided this and refuse to change my mind.

"What happened?" he asks, almost running into me as he grabs on to my arms and shakes me slightly. "It's bad, isn't it? It's bad. I took the blame. I told Dr. Brown everything. It was my fault. All of it."

I stare into his eyes, and my lips crack open in a wide smile.

"Oh god, you've lost it. Why are you smiling?" Everly nearly cries. He looks distraught. "Fine. You know what? I'll go down to Dr. Brown and tell him we've broken up. It's fine. We can just break up for a month and then we can get back together. You are not losing your job for me. It's decided."

"Everly," I begin, but he's pacing now, looking almost frantic. His hands are in his hair, tugging it, making it stick up in all directions.

"I mean, I might die because I won't survive not fucking you, or talking to you, or seeing you every day, but maybe we could just say we're broken up and keep spending the night together."

"Everly!" I nearly shout, and he stops moving.

"What?"

"It's fine. Dr. Brown said it's fine. We just need to keep it here and private. All PDA needs to stop until you graduate."

He lets out a long breath and nods. "Oh. Oh, okay. I can so do that. I can."

I let out a relieved laugh and then rub my hand across my mouth. "Yeah. It's going to be fine."

Everly nods, letting out a long breath. "Fine. It's going to be fine."

Cora Rose

He blinks and then grins and rushes toward me, picking me up and carrying me to the bedroom. "Fuck yes. Let's celebrate."

Chapter Nineteen

Everly

Silas is riding my dick, like really riding it. Like his life depends on it.

I mean, it kind of does. His life and mine.

If I don't come in his ass, I will probably die.

"Oh fuck, your dick is amazing. I've been thinking about it all day," Silas groans as he arches his hips forward, making me gasp. "Your dick and your ass."

"Me too. I couldn't stop thinking about it," I moan as my fingers dig into his hips.

He gasps when I sit up, changing our positions and impaling him deeper. Our lips meet in a frantic kiss.

"And kissing you. I couldn't stop thinking about this." He groans into me, his ass clenching around my hard length. Oh fuck, if he keeps doing that I'm going to burst early. And I don't want to come until he does.

But the way he's canting his hips and the way he feels around me makes it very hard.

Oh fuck, I'm so hard.

And he's currently auditioning to be a rodeo rider.

"Touch yourself," I say, but Silas just shakes his head.

"No. I can come untouched."

"I know you can," I wheeze. "But I'm not going to last."

"You can. You have to."

"I can't, Silas. You feel too good."

He moans and then shoves me backward. I fall onto my back and look up at him as he pulls off of me and straddles me reverse cowboy.

"Is this better?" he asks as he sucks my cock back into his hole.

"Well fuck," I gasp. "No, this is worse." Because now I can see his ass swallowing my dick. The sight of it, the feel...my balls draw up, and I fuck into him roughly, making him cry out.

On a shout, I come, uncontrolled, unbidden, filling him up and watching as my cum leaks from him and down my shaft.

Silas is panting when I'm done, my body still beneath his.

"Did you come? Fuck, sorry about that. It was too good."

Silas nods, his body pulling off mine.

"Yeah, I did. That position nailed my prostate just right."

I grin up at him and hold my arms out. He slides into them and nuzzles into my neck.

"One more week until graduation," he says, and I nod, holding him even closer.

"One more week until you can take me on a proper date."

He sighs and kisses the underside of my jaw.

"A proper date for my very improper boyfriend."

I chuckle as I press my nose into his hair. "Very improper. Just for you."

"What are your plans after graduation?" Silas asks, and I close my eyes, trying not to fall asleep. It's late, it's been a long day, and fuck, that orgasm is going to put me right to bed. But first, to answer his question.

Full Service

"Well, you could come by the strip club anytime you want and I could give you a private lap dance."

"I think I may. Or you could quit."

"I'll quit once I find a better job."

"I could take care of you."

"I won't be a kept man, Dr. Sinclair."

He huffs in frustration and nuzzles into my neck.

"But in all seriousness," I begin. "I thought we could go up north and you could meet my dad. We could take Grandpa too."

"Mm, that would be nice."

"And then I thought we could take a nice long, leisurely road trip back down the coast to home."

"Sounds lovely."

"And then, you know, you could ask me to move in."

I hold my breath as Silas leans up, his eyes meeting mine. "You've already moved in."

I shrug, trying to be casual. "Yeah, but not like permanently."

His head cocks. "I thought this *was* permanent."

"I figured that you were going to ask me to move out after graduation."

Silas snorts loudly. "Fuck that. I wasn't. Not ever."

"Oh," I say, blinking rapidly. "Well, that's a relief."

"It is. I just figured I'd keep you."

My heart stutters in my chest.

"Keep me?"

"Yes. Keep you."

I nod and then lean up, kissing him softly. "I think I'd like that."

Epilogue

Silas

I'm so incredibly nervous about meeting Everly's dad. I don't know why, but what if he hates me? What if he thinks I'm too old for his son? What if he thinks I suck?

I do suck sometimes.

Even though Everly doesn't seem to think so.

"You'll be fine," Lee says, reaching up and patting my shoulder. We're almost there, about twenty minutes away, and I think Lee's noticed I've stopped breathing. To be fair, I've been hyperventilating this entire trip. Eight hours in to this drive and I'm nearly dead. I'm going to need oxygen when I arrive.

How fitting.

"He's going to love you. I love you, so he will too," Lee says, and I find myself blinking hard to hold back tears.

"Stop being so sappy, Lee," I snap. "I don't want to show up crying. That will make a terrible impression."

Everly chuckles next to me. "Silas, it's going to be fine. Dad is super excited to meet my boyfriend. He's been looking forward to this all week. He even shaved so he looks presentable."

"Oh god. I didn't shave," I wheeze and rub at my scruffy face.

"Don't worry. You look hot with a beard, and I love the burn it gives me between my thighs."

I gasp at him and then throw my thumb over my shoulder. "Your grandpa is right there!"

"He's fine. He can't hear me."

Lee cackles. "I can hear just fine, Junior. Just fine indeed."

I sink down in my seat and cross my arms over my chest. "Fucking great."

Everly is still chuckling when we pull into the RV park and stop the car in front of a small trailer. A man, who resembles an older Everly is waiting outside, his hands in the pockets of his worn jeans, his hair combed neatly.

Hm, if this is what Everly will look like in the future, I've really outdone myself.

God, I'm a lucky guy.

"There he is. You ready?" Everly asks, and I shake my head.

"I think I'll just meet him here. He can come say hello through the window."

Everly shakes his head as he gets out of the car and makes his way to the passenger side door. His dad is already here, helping Lee out of the car, and when Everly pulls my door open, I nearly fall into his arms.

He's going to have to hold me up while I meet his father.

I can stand in front of hundreds of students and give a complicated lecture, but meeting Everly's dad is going to make me faint. My knees can't hold me up any longer. The bones have evaporated.

"Hello, Silas. I'm Joe," his dad says, holding out his hand. "Everly's told me so much about you."

Full Service

I nod and then squeak out a greeting before clearing my throat. "Same. I've been so excited to finally meet you."

Everly beams at me and then throws an arm around his dad. Honestly, I'll say it again. If this is what Everly is going to look like when he's older I won't survive it.

His dad is hot.

"Stop ogling my dad," Everly whispers into my ear as we start to follow his dad toward the trailer. "It's making me jealous."

My cheeks heat, and I shove at him lightly. "I'm not ogling. I'm just imagining you in twenty years."

"You like what you see?"

"Yes."

"Hm, that's good because I plan on seeing you in twenty years too."

"I'll make a very sad picture when compared to you."

He snorts a laugh. "No, I doubt that. You're the hottest man alive."

"I may be dead by then," I counter, and he shakes with laughter.

"You're such a fucking negative Nancy. Come on. Dad wants to talk to you."

"Oh god."

"Nothing bad, just wants to get to know my man. Never brought anyone home before."

"Really?"

He nods and kisses my cheek as we make our way over to the camping chairs Joe and Lee are perched on.

"Yeah, you're my first. My only."

My feet stop moving, and I glance over at him. "First and only?"

His cheeks flush pink. "Yeah, you know, because I..." He lets out a small huff. "I love you."

I blink at him, my mouth dropping open. "What did you just say?"

He shrugs like it's no big deal. "I love you."

"And you're telling me this now!? Right before I chat with your dad?"

"Yeah, you know, just so you know that this is serious."

I glower at him and then grab him and kiss him roughly. "I'm going to get you back for this. You love me and you tell me now. Good God, Everly."

He nods. "I mean, do you love me too? You can say it back, you know?"

I stare at him, at that perfect face, at the way he looks at me so softly. "Of course I do. I love you Everly Winslow-O'Conner. I've loved you for a while now."

"Really?"

"Yes. Now let's go talk to your dad. I need to woo him so when I ask you to marry me, he'll give his approval."

Now it's Everly's turn to stand there, shocked and confused.

Well, good.

It's what he deserves.

My future husband.

* * *

Thanks so much for reading Full Service.

If you're curious about Austin from the coffee cart, make sure to grab his story, Tongue-Tied.

Want more from me?
If you're looking for more college guys with a bit of obsession and stalker vibes the Unexpected Series is for you.

Full Service

If you're interested in keeping up with my releases join my newsletter here or join my Facebook group!

Meet all of the couples from FU2!

Perry and Theo
The Hookup Mix-up

Harrison and Benny
A Stealthy Situation

Blaise and Jordan
Batting Style

Jay and Ryan
Level Up

Silas and Everly
Full Service

Dex and Austin
Tongue-Tied

Chase and Amos
Method Acting

Emmett and Jonah
Twincerely Yours

About the Author

Cora Rose loves any kind of romance and consumes way too many books each year. She currently lives in the U.S. and spends her days daydreaming about the characters inside her head.

Also by Cora Rose

The Unexpected Series

Whit

Sem

Emery

Luke

Lex

Colin

Diablo

Ben

The Inevitable Series

Until Him

Always Him

Timeless Series

A Minute More

One More Time

Our Exception Series

Except You

Suddenly You

Standalone

Waiting for You

Exception

Cora Rose and Nicole Dykes

Behind the Camera Series

Reaching Reed

Becoming Bennet

Discovering Damon

Homegrown Hearts

Sunshine For Sale

Printed in Great Britain
by Amazon